COME THE WINTER

Vanessa Meredith, transferred from her prestigious position of under-secretary by the boss's snooping son Dominic, is now secretary to a famous, unpredictable thriller writer. Finally meeting at a party, Dominic has a fascination for Vanessa. Yet he shies away from love and marriage, and Vanessa must work out the puzzle for herself.

ELISABETH ARTHUR

COME THE WINTER

Complete and Unabridged

LINFORD
Leicester

First published in Great Britain in 1989 by
Robert Hale Limited
London

First Linford Edition
published October 1991
by arrangement with
Robert Hale Limited
London

British Library CIP Data

Arthur, Elisabeth *1917 –*
    Come the winter. — Large print ed. —
    Linford romance library
    I. Title
    813.54

    ISBN 0–7089–7103–2

Published by
F. A. Thorpe (Publishing) Ltd.
Anstey, Leicestershire
Set by Words & Graphics Ltd.
Anstey, Leicestershire
Printed and bound in Great Britain by
T. J. Press (Padstow) Ltd., Padstow, Cornwall

1

IT had been a gruelling interview and Vanessa Meredith escaped from Dominic Russell's office feeling frustrated and furious. In the end, because she was rebellious he'd given her the sack. True she'd been offered another job but, in her hurt resentment, she'd turned it down, spiting herself and not scoring a point.

Nothing to read from his expression, he'd said coolly: "Suit yourself. Goodbye Miss Meredith. Collect your belongings and salary to the end of the month."

Vanessa reached the office she shared with his secretary and collapsed into her chair, staring blankly at the unfinished work on the chaotic desk. As if her wandering curiously into the secret recesses of the security department hadn't been blasted enough, he had criticised her poor punctuality and lamentable arrears with work, home truths she loved him even less for. He was an arrogant pig, she decided, and, inwardly condemned the Russells' organisation to blazes.

Tracy Holt came in, lean and immaculate, just like her detestable boss. She sat at her own tidy desk and, like the automaton she was, began work immediately. To Vanessa she said: "It's no use moping, you knew the penalty for breaking the rules."

"I suppose he told you?"

"I'm to type your official dismissal."

Put in these terms, the finality was awful. Dismissal . . . and from a prestige post about which she had boasted to her sister and stepfather: under-secretary to the boss, or rather to the boss's son although that was inconsequential, Mr John Russell keeping a low profile, poring over his secret weapons no doubt.

Her sense of injustice fading, Vanessa said: "The barrier was open so I — "

"No excuse. Like you, the guard is

out and he gets no pay."

"But — "

"It's in his contract. I suppose you haven't read yours?"

In a cursory fashion. Vanessa shuffled some of the scattered letters together, a brick in her stomach at the mention of money. She and her flat-mate, both extravagant, lived on a permanent shoe-string. Living in London was expensive. She would have to crawl home and poor Adrienne would never manage to keep on the flat.

After a great deal of heart-searching, Vanessa decided it was better to crawl to an arrogant pig than to a smirking told-you-so stepfather. And she didn't want to go home for more reasons than one.

Self-mocking but still weak from the searing interview, Vanessa sent up a brief memorandum and received an equally terse one in reply: "I'll be in touch after hours."

A floor above, in his own office, Dominic Russell flicked the incoming memo into the waste-basket. Impudent little devil, memos were strictly for department heads. Leaning back in his chair, he eyed the in-tray without enthusiasm. He was dog-tired, escaping from one battle into another, in no mood to deal with recalcitrant employees. But what a girl, that pale skin and fiery hair. Shame she had to go. Unpunctuality he might put right, cheek he certainly would, but snooping was something he couldn't overlook.

Vanessa hadn't expected 'after hours' to mean a lift home and, when the long, black monster of a car drew up at the bus stop, she turned her back. What it was that made her obey the authoritative voice and the six-foot male taking her decisively by the arm and deftly inserting her into the luxurious comfort of the passenger seat she couldn't define, but as the car drew expertly into the teeming traffic, she panicked.

"Where are you taking me?" she demanded.

"To your destination."

"How do you know where I live?"

"According to the bus stop."

"I'm not going home."

Dominic said impatiently: "Liar too. I had your address sent up to me. D'you imagine me a fool?"

No, Vanessa didn't, but she imagined him ruthless and that did nothing to still the rapidity of her heartbeats. Gossip was rife amongst the staff and his reputation wasn't reassuring. How stupidly she'd fallen into his trap. Hadn't the rape of her sister been a lesson enough?

Vanessa fumbled for the door handle and he said calmly: "The exits and seat-belts are electrically controlled, Miss Meredith. By me. Just sit still until we are out of the traffic. Then we'll talk if you can control your imagination long enough to be rational."

A skilful driver, he drew up outside the house in record time, giving the dilapidated exterior a swift, frowning glance before turning his enquiring blue gaze to her tightly controlled face.

"Tell me about yourself, Vanessa Meredith."

"If you saw my dossier you must know all there is to know."

He said thoughtfully: "Twenty-two years of age. Blue eyes. Chestnut hair. Five feet six. Slim build. Excellent references. Character details: Quick-tempered . . . Allergic to men . . . especially those like me . . . "

Vanessa struggled to control her temper, knowing he was being deliberately provocative. "I don't know you well enough to have any opinion of you, Mr Russell."

"Only by hearsay. Actually I meant you are allergic to authority, Miss Meredith."

She said swiftly: "My stepfather is a bossy pig."

"So you ran away from a bossy pig."

"I left home in a perfectly civilised manner."

His grunt spoke louder than words, making her seethe. He observed without expression: "Not according to your sister and guardian."

She gripped her fingers together, regaining a hard-won composure and determined not to be indiscreet. After all she needed a job badly and was, for the moment, entirely in his hands. Managing a creditable calmness, she said: "His reference means nothing to me. He lost a general dogsbody, and Janie, she lost my support." Suddenly tired of the cat and mouse she tugged at the seat-belt, feeling trapped: "Please let me out of here. It may amuse you to conduct a further interrogation, but *I* have had enough. I'm tired and I'm hungry." To her mortification she heard the tremor in her voice: "I thought we were going to discuss another position with someone you know."

The belt was released with a deft touch of a switch and he said in obvious sincerity: "Sorry. It wasn't my intention to keep you fastened-in and, regarding the post, I haven't contacted my friend yet, haven't had time. However I've fixed a meal for tonight hoping you are both free. If not we'll make it another time although that might be some weeks ahead. Are you free?"

A meal! Vanessa thought of the sausages allocated for the evening, and of Adrienne who was permanently hungry, and of the times she'd acted hostess for her stepfather. Her taste-buds watered treacherously.

He was sitting patiently, waiting for a reply and she glanced up at her flat-mate's pale face pressed curiously to the window. Impulsively, Vanessa said: "It's useless me trying to be independent; have you ever been in this situation, Mr Russell?" Not giving him time to reply and not wanting one, she went on: "I am free. I don't venture out alone after dark. But I can't leave Adrienne to eat sausages."

He laughed and it was infectious. Vanessa found herself laughing with him.

"Bring Adrienne along too," he said — "and if you don't hear to the contrary I'll pick you up at eight o'clock."

Vanessa unloaded the whole of the day's events on the fascinated Adrienne, not embroidering Dominic Russell's attitude despite their amiable conclusion. "He's not a man to be underestimated," she finished a trifle diffidently. "If he didn't have a sense of humour he'd be downright frightening."

Adrienne wasn't interested in Dominic Russell's characteristics. Villain or not he was the means of a meal and an outing. Abandoned as a child and brought up in a foster home, she could not understand Vanessa's illusions or her astonishing beliefs in the human race. True, her flatmate had suffered anguish over the affair with her sister but Adrienne had to stifle indifference. Janie had been raped. So what? Wasn't that happening to girls everyday?

"Ah Dominic, you're back from the

frozen wastes," George Vernon said into the telephone. "When are you joining us?"

"Can't say. Have to go about some unfinished business. I want you to do something for me. Take a girl off my hands, and, my dear imaginative idiot, it's not what your lurid mind is conjuring up. A secretary you badly need in that wild establishment of ours, one who'll fit in beautifully and is able, I believe, to turn a hand to anything. Keep her away from Father for the time being, and don't waste time protesting. You'll have her and like it."

"I'm not one of your employees, thank the Lord, you bossy devil. What's she like, this woman of yours?"

"I've told you, useful."

"To look at?"

"What does that matter? I met her for the first time today."

"I'm suspicious. What's the problem?"

"Just take her and stop wasting precious time. Will you meet Vanessa

Meredith and me for a meal around eight tonight?"

"So her name's Vanessa. Very classy. And no, I won't meet you, I'm busy like you. I'll send Fabian . . . and Dom, you swine, I'll give you hell when you do condescend to come. It's been six weeks or haven't you noticed?"

"I've noticed . . . Missed my beautiful hills . . . and you of course . . . at least I think so."

He rang off with several unprintable adjectives warming his ears.

Adrienne searched her scanty wardrobe and came up with a long, black skirt and flimsy cream blouse, her rounded breasts clearly visible: "Will I do?"

Vanessa, her system churning at the thought of the coming outing, merely replied vaguely about the absence of a bra. Her doubts were multiplying alarmingly. She knew little about the father and son for whom she'd been working, had given no thought to their activities despite the rigorous vetting of her integrity and the necessity of so many references. Obtaining a prestige position as under-secretary to a flourishing organisation had put her on a cloud nine where suppositions didn't penetrate. It was, after all, her first venture into the big-business world. Over the weeks she had heard and absorbed rumours on the grapevine, these all promptly sniffed at by the knowledgeable Tracy Holt, who disregarded anything she didn't know about as rubbish.

Vanessa had blithely accepted, happy, unencumbered for the first time by family, and at last, with such a generous salary, independent. And like a brainless fool she had wandered into an unguarded cellar and seen a spanking new machine that looked like something from outer space.

Adrienne was chattering away, pathetically excited and blatantly nervous. And that, Vanessa thought grimly, makes two of us. Why did I let myself in for an evening with my ex-boss knowing I'll be beaten to pulp if I don't let him have his way? Humour came to the rescue as she remembered one of the younger employee's comment regarding the Russells: "It's not," the fresh-faced Tony Pelham had whispered in her ear, "vee have vays of making you talk. It's vee have vays of extracting loyalty and obedience. Sign here."

She had laughed at the time.

"He's here." Adrienne was, once more, decorating the window. An apt description, her slight body tense with apprehensive excitement and her golden hair a bright halo in the fading rays of the sun. Voice pitched higher than normal, she exclaimed: "Wow, what a car, looks more like a hearse." Giggling at her own absurdity, she grabbed Vanessa's arm: "Watch over me and kick if I drop a clanger. I'll watch you with the cutlery, never learnt manners with the Foster, stood up to eat . . . too many of us to get round a table . . . "

Vanessa said fiercely: "Shut up. Get

it out of your head that you are inferior to people like the Russells. You're better than tycoons who tread on their employees. Be yourself. You're fine." But she did wish Adrienne had worn a bra and blamed herself for not insisting.

Despite her reservations and the absent bra, the evening went smoothly, Adrienne quiet but sparkling with appreciation, Dominic the suave, perfect host and Fabian Vernon, although less of a man than his friend, likable and sensitive. The venue was first-class, the food and wine excellent; there was no calculated move to refill glasses without consent. Vanessa would have been less than human not to have relaxed.

Discreetly observing the two men she concluded Dominic Russell's touch of arrogance was unconscious. He had hard, strong features, eyes that changed colour with his mood and a forbidding mouth belied by his sudden bursts of humour. Nevertheless, she didn't feel she was learning much about him and decided that 'iron in his soul' was an apt summary, confirming his harsh attitude to employees who broke the stringent rules of contract.

Fabian was easier to assess. Obviously a dreamer and all too obviously willing to please his stronger companion.

From him, Vanessa heard a smattering of Dominic's background, of their idyllic surroundings as children, over-the-top adventures and useless despair when holidays were over. Her own life before her father died had not been under-indulged but Dominic, it appeared, had been granted every whim. And that, she thought, made sense.

Dominic was a man who didn't discuss business at the table and the proposition of a post with the famous thriller writer, George Vernon, was put to Vanessa over coffee and liqueurs in the lounge. Adrienne exclaimed at the mention of the writer's name but Vanessa was unmoved, was merely vaguely familiar with his name and had never read any of his books. She was not an avid reader and had her own favourite authors. Alone with Dominic Russell she would have expressed in full what she thought about the proposal but, with Fabian present, the situation was delicate. Eyes clashing with those that were now steely grey, she asked coolly: "Why didn't you tell me about this scheme on the journey here, giving me time to think about it? I believe Mr Vernon lives in an isolated mansion and is given to occasional bursts of fury."

The grey turned to amused blue and, this time, Dominic gestured to the waiter to refill the glasses. Tone as cool as hers, he said: "Gossip, Miss Meredith. All the people at the top are subject to it."

"As you are?"

His lips twitched, but he was not to be drawn. "The house is rambling, hardly a mansion, and, as to isolation, there is plenty of transport available. I naturally assume such a capable young woman as yourself can drive a vehicle."

So he had shed his role as a perfect

host and was back to sniping. Vanessa glanced from Adrienne's puzzled stare to Fabian's frowning anxiety. He said in his gentle manner: "Please consider the job, Miss Meredith. Having met you I'm convinced you would be ideal. George and I need a fresh young face to bring us up to scratch." Proving he was not as guileless as he appeared, he added: "Dominic, stop tormenting. Miss Meredith is too much of a lady to answer as you deserve."

"And that," retorted Dominic, "is rubbish. During the short time I have spent with Miss Vanessa Meredith I have learned she is quite capable of dealing with me."

Two hours later, Adrienne lay on her back extolling the evening, while Vanessa shed a few angry tears into her pillow, at odds with the world. She had given way to coercion and would shortly leave London for an unknown future.

Adrienne said: "I'm too excited to sleep, I'll make some tea. Oh boy, what a fabulous time we've had." Her voice floated out of the tiny kitchen. "I think DR is a real man, frightening though, and his flat . . . out of this world. Not homely but breathtaking. Those pictures — were they genuine? Not that I go a bomb on that sort of thing . . . too highbrow. D'you want a biscuit or are you asleep?"

"No and no."

"You sound miffed."

"I'm tired." Vanessa sat up and accepted the mug. "It's been a heavy day. I feel steam-rollered."

"Are you worried about the new job?" Some of her ardour dampened, Adrienne gazed anxiously into her mentor's flushed face: "You don't have to go . . . can back off."

"And live on what?"

"Go home."

Vanessa set the mug on the floor and dived under the duvet, the conversation settling her indecision. Even letting the objectional demigod have his way was preferable to the last suggestion.

One concrete consolation out of the

whole sorry business was the human side of Dominic Russell in offering Adrienne a job in the typing pool. She, of course, would be too scared to snoop and, in any case, the pool was conveniently segregated from the works.

2

DESPITE her unease, Vanessa slept, and awoke to a nervously excited Adrienne, already dressed and eager to go to the office. In a tight navy skirt and snowy blouse, hair severely brushed, she looked ideally suited to the office pool and the astringent requirements of the Russell Foundation Company which, as yet, had resisted the battering-ram of larger competitors. The grapevine had produced numerous proposals; the Russells, father and son, stood grimly tight. But for how long? was now the question. Older employees, more loyal, shook wise heads. Who, in these days of every man for himself, would take on Mr Dominic's job?

Curiosity whetted, Vanessa had tried to discover just what Mr Dominic's job was and was baffled by the negative suggestions. He works abroad, appeared to be the standard answer.

Vanessa's own exodus, two days later, was unemotional; the regret she felt at losing her independence again and the volatile company of Adrienne, was secondary to the apprehension curdling her stomach and the overall feeling of being manipulated. Dominic Russell had pulled the strings and she was helpless to do anything but jump to his command. Epithets flooded her mind as she packed the last of her belongings.

Officious, strait-laced, coldly uncaring. How he had rammed her misdemeanours home, the righteous prig. Was he so perfect himself? Hadn't he expected her to retaliate? She slammed the last case shut. It had been frightening the way his eyes had changed from blue to slate-grey. Never would she forget the humiliation of that awful interview.

Trying to keep at bay the knowledge that she had asked for trouble, Vanessa made the last round of the flat to check everything was in order for the less capable Adrienne to cope with. That the girl could continue to live in comfort was a bonus and a relief. The salaries paid by the hierarchy were incredibly generous, one point in their favour. Payment for loyalty! Vanessa felt her cheeks burn and was still hot when she went down to fit herself into the snug seat of Fabian's low-slung sports car. Strangely, she felt no restraint with him but she wasn't looking forward to the meeting with her new employer, the prestigious crime writer, George Vernon.

Conversation was impossible over the roar of the powerful engine; Fabian drove, utterly relaxed, but with total disregard for anything else on the road. A hairy drive at great speed, all signs but traffic lights ignored. A quirk in the character of an otherwise considerate man.

There was no break for refreshment or any other reason, just a constant roar with the wind battering her face and tying her hair into knots.

Vanessa felt weak when they pulled up just inside a pair of impressive iron gates and Fabian, cutting the engine, turned to regard her tight expression with blatant guilt in his own.

"I forgot," he said with deep contrition, "Dominic told me not to burn up. Are you all right, Miss Meredith?"

"Coming round." To regain composure she feigned interest in the surroundings, noting the name, Hillside Manor, graphically inscribed on an oak surround. "Is this where you live?"

"Mostly." Still uncomfortable he waved an elegant hand at the tangle of shrubs: "Lost the gardener . . . died . . . old man . . . Dom's been too busy to replace him yet."

"I thought Mr Russell lived in Mayfair."

"Well, he does, with his father, mostly. At least . . . " He broke off, then finished lamely, "he prefers to be here. Likes the hills. Peaceful y'know . . . after travelling."

Vanessa took pity on him: "How far is the house from here? I'd rather like to go on."

"Half-a-mile, but if you could give me another minute I . . . " He fumbled for an unnecessary handkerchief and blew his nose, then rushed into speech: "Dom says you can turn your hand to anything. Er . . . can you cook?"

She stiffened defensively. "I was engaged as a secretary, not a domestic."

"Yes, well . . . " Disconcerted he said: "George isn't writing at the moment, just finished a book. We hoped you would join us as one of the family, do a bit of organising, if you know what I mean. We sort of muddle through and George hates domestics about. In a way we all pull together and we thought, for the time being, as there's no typing, you might . . . "

Vanessa inwardly squirmed with anger and bitterness. It was back to the grind, being a dogsbody, tackling all the work no one else wanted to do. If Dominic Russell had been within a stone's throw she'd have attacked him.

Fabian said unhappily: "There's one other thing I must tell you . . . about Dominic. George is fanatically possessive of him, can be foul about competition, has been since we were all kids. I — "

She cut him off, disgust in her voice: "I'm not interested in Mr Russell or any other man. All I want is to do my own work and, moreover, from now on, mind my own business. Mr Vernon, can we please go into the house."

He restarted the engine, running it slowly. "I've made a hash of things, wouldn't make a diplomat. When you've met George you'll — "

"Please," Vanessa begged, "I'm in agony. We'll sort things out later."

He drove on and the house came into view beyond a long line of golden laurels — a well-maintained house built of warm stone, with long windows opening on to a wide, clean patio, over which a glass roof protected the comfortable garden furniture and urns of exotic plants.

Vanessa momentarily forgot her discomfort and stared with pleasure at her future lodgings. No wonder the frigid demigod liked it here. Anyone would like it here. Turning her head she caught a glimpse of the hills he was professed to love, finding them breathtaking and mysterious, a parallel with him.

Fabian murmured: "There's George."

A woman, dragging a spade, gave a vague wave in their direction and he added apologetically: "Georgina, in reality, but she's used the man's name ever since she hit the jackpot, refuses to answer to any other. Except to Dominic, of course — he never gives way to eccentricities."

Her eyes on her future employer, Vanessa felt relief rather than shock: a joke at her expense. She asked: "Is he here often?"

"As often as he can be."

She could believe that, now Georgina Vernon was in full view: an astonishingly frail-looking woman with an abundance of long, fair hair, a guileless expression and a strange concoction of clothing that could not possibly be a sufficient shield against the cool, easterly breeze. In turn she eyed Vanessa then spoke into the air: "So he couldn't describe you, eh? For a man who despises liars he does a pretty good job himself." She assessed Vanessa once more then, with a nod that could mean anything, turned to her brother who was leaning on the car: "Get that stuff inside and let's eat. I've just buried a wretched cat that dived to suicide from an upstairs ledge. You must have shut it in your attic. And you, Vanessa, isn't it? Come and learn the geography if only to take that pained look off your face."

Following her into the house, Vanessa wondered why the woman used a man's name. There was nothing masculine about her.

Fabian had understated when he'd mentioned a lack of routine. Meals were when Georgina felt hungry and there were no organised hours of work, either for writing or for housework. A sullen girl appeared twice a week from out of the unknown, cleaned wearily and disappeared at no given hour. To Vanessa, used to six months of the rat-race, life, seemingly shut away miles from civilisation, became strangely unreal. The Vernons lifestyle was unbelievable. Had it not been for the need of grovelling to her stepfather, the lack of, as yet, unpaid salary and the unending curiosity she possessed, Vanessa would have slipped away, her humour bubbling at the conviction that she would scarcely be missed.

But the weather was fine and the surroundings breathtakingly beautiful. She gardened and tried not to think about Dominic Russell, doing whatever in foreign countries.

Fabian was a sketch artist. He could gaze absently at a subject, sit with his elegant back turned and produce a perfect likeness within minutes. He was also a picture script writer. Mostly he worked in the conservatory, almost obliterated by overgrown ferns and hanging baskets crammed with rioting fuchsias. He told Vanessa he never drew flora, fauna sometimes, but mainly people, silly people or lovely, young girls who were in love.

"One day I might paint your picture, but not yet, the time isn't ripe." He sketched Adrienne, a wonderful likeness, capturing her basic simplicity under the assumed maturity. Vanessa sent it to her erstwhile flatmate thus breaking her isolation, hoping for a phone call and receiving one two days later as she waited in the big hall for a shower to pass. Patiently waiting for Adrienne's enthusiasm over the portrait, her new job, and a second date with the same man to subside, Vanessa, at last, asked about the boss.

"He's in and out. A bit scary. Doesn't speak to any of us lesser mortals. But he's some fella, Vannie, all the girls swoon over him. I was sent to his office once, but it was as if he'd never seen me before. He just looked furious when he read the telex but it didn't make sense to me; some sort of code, I guess. I did think he might have recognised me and asked how I was getting on, or even about you."

Vanessa laughed: "Why ever should he? I'll bet he's forgotten our existence. I'm in seclusion and you're a mere pooley." To the other girl's avid questioning she was cautious. Adrienne was a chatterbox. Cutting the lengthy call to a halt, Vanessa warned about using the firm's telephone, perhaps blocking an important communication — one of the many rules imposed on employees.

Noting automatically that the boundary fence needed repair, Dominic climbed the steep path towards the first flat platform, his place of refuge. He had skirted the house, leaving his car under the laurels, wanting to be alone to relax for a few hours. Every inch of his six-foot frame ached with tension and his mind would not part from the sight of his colleague throwing up his arms before collapsing to add a pool of blood to the already stained ground. No use telling himself Paxton had asked for it, belting off in panic. The man had left a wife and four children and Mrs Paxton's reception of the tragedy had been hysterically vitriolic. "Murder! You let him be murdered," she'd said.

Dominic stopped. He was out of breath, not out of training. He felt sick with the whole damned affair. No way was he going to be successful with that doomed machine, despite his father's conviction. For himself he would let it go. Impossible for the gun-happy fanatics to discover the intricate usage. He was the only one who knew and he wished he didn't.

She was lying on his spot, the girl who had upset the smooth running of Russell and Son, Computer Engineers. He stood staring down at her, angry yet unable to stem appreciation. Different from the girls he dated, she was maddeningly irritating, fiery like that gorgeous hair, proud as the silly, upturned nose and, in sleep, vulnerable. He wanted to pitch her over the cliff.

Instead he sat down beside her and leaned back against the crooked tree, age-old, the silver stripped from its trunk by the prevailing wind.

Opening her eyes to see a chunk of seething male close beside her was a shock. Vanessa blinked, looked again and said faintly: "Help."

He gave her a fleeting glance.

"Did you come up or down?" Vanessa asked.

"Up as a matter of fact."

"That makes sense."

"You, young Meredith, have usurped my spot."

"So sorry sir. I'll move . . . "

As she made to do so his fingers gripped her wrist: "Don't be so bloody-minded. If you are overworked and have to sleep during the day, go back to sleep."

"Boredom."

"I assume you don't drive?"

"As if you didn't know that when you had me incarcerated."

"You came of your own free will."

"If you believe that I doubt your intelligence."

"Impudent." He passed the comment absently, without rancour.

"You aren't my boss any more. I don't like being humiliated. You don't know what you did to me."

"And you'll never know what you did to me." Dominic eased his shoulders, his attention on the distant mist-swept hills. Without expression he said: "This bickering is childish."

"I agree." Vanessa gave a little tug and he released her wrist, turning his head to meet the hostility in her eyes, his own clouded and unreadable.

"Are you unhappy here?"

Vanessa shook her head. "This place gets a hold but I hate being idle. The Vernons really don't need me."

"A different version from what I've heard. Organising maniac, I understand from Georgina. No complaints however. I noticed the garden too."

"I take out my frustration on the soil."

Out of the blue, he asked: "Have you worked on computers?"

"Yes."

"You didn't say so at your interview."

"One only answers questions when being interrogated."

His eyes were very dark. "A sobering thought. One would have to be a fool or a hero not to . . . " Standing up he looked down at her: "I'm overstaying the time I had to spare. Do me a favour and forget you've seen me."

"Yes." For some reason, Vanessa felt depressed. "And I won't take your spot again."

"Feel free. It's rare I have the time to come on a stolen visit. Keep up the good work and keep Georgina in order. You should make a good pair, both wilful."

Vanessa watched him go, noting his light step. Perhaps the brief interlude had done him good, despite her invasion.

Half an hour later, Fabian met her in the hall, waving a recipe book at her. "George caught Dominic trying to sneak off and she's furious with him. I'm cooking a special meal to heal the breach . . . an order actually. He says you aren't a skivvy. As if we ever thought so, but . . . well . . . when Dom says jump I usually do . . . always did . . . can't help it. He's got that something."

Vanessa knew what he meant. She tossed her jacket on the oak bench. "I can't go on being idle. I've got to do something. When do I sight a manuscript?"

"You'll know. Any minute now you'll be snowed under and I'll be turfed out of the conservatory while George murders her latest victim." As he moved towards the kitchen he said with puckish mischief: "I marvel he gave way. He doesn't usually. Maybe there's an added attraction."

Vanessa didn't ask him what he meant.

Wondering where Dominic was, Vanessa ran up the wide staircase to her sumptuous bedroom. Feeling a twinge of nervousness she stripped off her crumpled clothes and went thankfully into the bathroom. All the rooms in the house were lavishly appointed, the six major bedrooms *en suite*. Insatiable curiosity had taken her into the empty ones and she knew Dominic occupied the third along the corridor. The wardrobe was full of expensive clothes and on the dressing-table was an enlarged photograph of Georgina. Across the bottom, in flamboyant style, was written: 'To my beloved hero. Love you ever. George.'

Vanessa felt sick whenever she thought of the misleading signature. Guessing the meal would be at a reasonable hour if Dominic had to leave, she showered and dressed quickly, brushing her hair with vigour and fastening it in a neat bun at the back. The dress she chose was of soft green wool with a calf-length skirt that swung as she walked, a clever touch of rust at the neckline complementing her colouring. It was a dress of demure simplicity and she disliked it heartily, but it had cost the earth and she felt, in her reduced circumstances, she must get some wear out of the wretched garment. It reminded her of the days she wanted to forget. Those under the jurisdiction of her stepfather after the awful assault on Janie. He had forbidden 'suggestive clothing', actually blaming the rape on the sun-top and too short skirt. But Janie had been a mere child and the man . . . Vanessa forced her mind back to the present knowing it was time she put the whole traumatic affair behind. It was an easy resolution to make, but not so easy to keep.

As she went down the wide, curving staircase, Vanessa eyed appreciatively her own handiwork. She had turned the higgledy-piggledy confusion into a comfortable lounge-hall, restoring a continuity of colour and a pattern to the placing of the valuable oil paintings. Her favourite, a Gainsborough, depicting his conception of the youthful innocence of a child long ago, was set in the prime position over the massive, open fireplace.

Dominic was looking at it, dark head slightly tilted, a position that accentuated the strong line of his profile. Vanessa paused and, for the first time, wondered what part he played in this cosmopolitan establishment. Was he part-owner or simply a welcome guest? If the former, maybe he would disapprove of her renovations as he had every right to do. The Vernons seemed not to have noticed any change. Perhaps she should ask him.

As she covered the last few stairs he turned to watch until she came fully into view. Then he made a mocking bow.

"My, my, young woman, a big hat, some padding, a fuller flounce and you could be Gainsborough's naïve idea of unsullied purity. Who hung the painting in the place of honour?"

Mortified at the colour burning her cheeks, Vanessa said stiffly. "I did. Do you object, Mr Russell?"

"No." He stared at her, brows arched. "Why so formal? I thought we'd called a truce."

She felt stupidly at a loss: "Yes, well . . . " Her flush crept maddeningly to her brow.

Dominic made an impatient gesture: "Come and have a drink. God knows what Fabian is cooking up or whether Georgina will come out of hiding. She's sulking under the greenery. How have you coped with her moods?"

As far as Vanessa knew there had been no moods. Slowly she followed Dominic into the smaller of the two sitting-rooms most frequented by the family. He was standing near the big, floor-length window, the day's newspaper spread between his hands. Against her better judgement, Vanessa's attention focused appreciatively on his long, lean, frame clad in a dark lightweight suit that appeared to have been poured over him. She failed to understand why a man who appeared to be relaxed in body could frown with such ferocity at whatever he was reading.

Flinging the paper aside with a sudden move of disgust he caught sight of her startled expression and gave his infectious laugh: "Morons, the lot of 'em," he said — "do you suffer fools gladly, young Meredith?"

"No . . . and my name is Vanessa."

Ignoring the rebuke he asked: "Do you consider me a fool?"

"No. Not a fool."

"I suspect an underlying reservation in those starchy tones. All my friends do, even my father or, at least, he takes me for one. What *do* you think of me?"

Vanessa walked to the cabinet, deliberately swinging her skirt: "I don't think of you at all now I've got over the initial dislike. What do you want to drink?"

He was at her side in a second,

fingers tight over her shoulder. In his unconsciously arrogant tone, he said: "Pouring drinks is a man's job."

"Not in this house it isn't."

"While I'm here it is."

With a quick shrug she freed herself from his grip, the annoyance she expected to feel bubbling into amusement. "We're bickering again, Sir Demi-god. Keep your hands to yourself."

"Suddenly I can't, young Meredith. I want to kiss you. I find myself enslaved by your contempt for me. What d'you say?"

Vanessa stood motionless. Now was her chance to carry out the resolution, put the fear of a man's proximity to the test. She could actually feel his breath penetrating her hair and touching her neck. No revulsion. Yet he was as capable of raping a woman as the brute who had assaulted Janie. Then, devastatingly, the revulsion came. This was a virile man and sex was a male priority. An embrace wouldn't stop at a kiss.

The shudder shook her from head to foot and Dominic said abruptly: "This fixation will ruin your life. Do you rate all men alike. Try to put a little intelligence into your thinking. What do you want to drink?"

Her voice husky in the back of her throat, Vanessa said weakly: "Martini . . . dry."

"Ice and lemon?"

"Yes." Normality bringing resentment at his cavalier treatment, she added: "I've been warned to avoid Georgina's claws."

Surprisingly, he patted her bottom: "A good try, my child. Game to the end. I'd still like to kiss you. Maybe there'll be a later date but I'm not too sure of that."

Vanessa felt tired of innuendoes. "Why? Fabian says you will spend the winter months here."

"Maybe. I don't know. If I'm not abroad."

The strange chill she felt was entirely different from the clamming coldness of revulsion. Astonishing herself she blurted: "You can kiss me if you like. It's not important. Is it?"

He took the glass from her and set it down: "Perhaps. Perhaps not. Shall we find out."

Now she felt the urge to cowardly retreat but his hands were firm about her face. Softly he commanded: "Close your eyes — I want to look at you — and relax, girl, relax, I'm not about to take liberties. Know what, Vanessa Meredith, I wish I'd never come into contact with you. I've enough on my back without a novice." As she tried to pull away he kissed her, his hands sliding down to hold her shoulders. A chaste kiss, or was it, she hardly knew. All she knew was that there was a depth in it that took her breath away.

"Well?" Now his eyes were very blue. "Any warmer?" The question was compassionate but he spoiled the reassurance by adding: "In a way you are right about men. We're a pretty loathsome breed with not much to choose between us. Better for you to crawl back into your shell and stay there but . . . with this hair . . . " He pushed her away: "We are about to be invaded so grab a little composure; you look delightfully bemused, but we'll keep that a secret."

She hadn't heard Fabian's approach. Obediently she picked up her glass and took a rashly generous drink, then turned swiftly from Dominic's amused gaze, not understanding him in the least. Why should he have asked to kiss her!

His face flushed with resentment, Fabian erupted into the room waving a wooden spoon: "She won't come," he said. "Dominic, you've got to do something about it. My lovely, lovely meal. It's an insult. It's heartbreaking. Make her come."

Dominic said lazily: "Oh, let her stew. We'll eat without her."

"You don't understand . . . the meal's for four. The table is set for four. There must be four. Dom . . . "

44

Dominic put down his glass: "Well don't cry about it. Have a drink and calm down. I'll see what I can do."

Fabian visibly relaxed. "He can always make her see reason. Trouble is she's got her teeth into a novel and from now on will be hell to live with — "

He went on speaking but Vanessa's attention was on Dominic. He had given way but his jaw had hardened, and she wondered why he objected to such a simple request when Georgina's partiality towards him was so blatantly obvious. He was, she thought, very tigerish with his long, easy stride and perfect co-ordination of muscle and strength. Her stomach tightened painfully as she recalled his words of warning. Men are pretty loathsome, there isn't much to choose between us. They were, her thoughts ran on, frighteningly strong too and even more frighteningly able to get their own way.

He came back with Georgina clinging

to his arm. Her eyes strangely golden, she said: "What a fuss over nothing, darlings. Give me one good reason why I should be torn from creation to satisfy your bellies? I'm not hungry. Dom, my darling . . . " she weaved an arm around his neck and kissed his taut cheek, "save me from the media."

He disentangled himself: "Go and put a decent dress on, something feminine."

Georgina's golden eyes narrowed over Vanessa's attire. "There's no competition."

Fabian said sharply: "Just because your heroine is a bitch there's no need for you to act the part."

"Oh, but there is, it's true characterisation. One must act . . . Dom agrees with me, don't you precious?" She grabbed at him again, kissing him passionately on the mouth while one hand ruffled his hair into wild confusion. "You love me, don't you? I might marry you one day, you've asked me often enough. Anyhow, darling, my bedroom door will be open tonight, and I feel in need of inspiration." With a wicked smile all round she made a dramatic exit, her shapeless white robe floating behind her.

"Dear heaven," Fabian exclaimed, "she's in one of those moods. I hope you'll satisfy her, Dominic, or life won't be worth living."

Dominic was straightening his hair with angry fingers but at this outrageous request he broke into his spontaneous laugh: "You damned fool, have you forgotten Vanessa is here. She won't understand this Bohemian byplay. Just pipe down and pour some drinks while I go and tidy up." He paused to study her tight face, then added: "I might just satisfy Georgina now and then we can all have a meal in peace."

After he had gone, Vanessa tipped back her second Martini and accepted another. She felt isolated and stupid, not knowing how much to take seriously. There was truth in what Dominic termed the byplay, but how much she couldn't guess. Meeting Fabian's sympathetic glance she asked: "Are they in love with each other or is that an act?"

He moved his shoulders uncomfortably: "To be honest, I don't know. George is unpredictable and Dom isn't a man who shows what he feels. He was reared the hard way and never confided even when we were kids together." He also tipped back his drink and had a refill. "She mothered us in her way and it was a novelty to Dom coming from an all-male household. His father won't employ females, not in the home." Seeing Vanessa's astonished expression, he enlarged: "Surely you know what happened when Dom was a child? His father made off with John Russell's wife, leaving Dominic behind."

"But . . . he calls the boss Father."

"He has to. He was legally adopted. No sentiment in it though. Just a duty."

3

VANESSA woke with a start to find no sign of daylight seeping through the curtains. Her nightdress was revoltingly damp round her neck and shoulders, her heart thumping painfully and all the signs of a hangover clamping her head.

Crawling from the bed she weaved into the bathroom to take a shower, deliberately suffering under an icy downpour. Serve her right. Stupid to let her wine glass be refilled each time she took a sip. And three Martinis. Shades of the past, more than the water, made her shudder. Her mother had been an alcoholic.

But her feeling of sickness was more than that. Wrapped in a towel, she parted the curtains and sat on the window seat, head in hands, striving for common sense. He had visited the room next door, satisfying Georgina, leaving without caution and whistling his way along the passage to slam his own door. Damn him!

She calmed down after a while, watching the day struggle into a grey existence. What Dominic Russell did was no concern of hers; Georgina was his mistress. So what? That meant nothing these days. What was really shaming was her own inhibited outlook.

Several coffees later, Vanessa came up from the kitchen and found the door to Dominic's room wide open. He had gone. Expecting to see chaos, she entered to find the room immaculate, and as she drew aside the curtains she remembered the conversation with Fabian. Her curiosity aroused, she had pressed for more information, learning that Dominic's mother had died as she gave him life and that the man who had adopted him was his father's brother.

Dominic had left a note on her breakfast plate. No beginning, no ending. "You are now in for a gruelling time, young Meredith. I've quietened the great novelist for you . . . for a time. Don't let the implication paralyse your Puritan instincts. Best of luck."

He was right about the gruelling time. In the weeks that followed, Vanessa marvelled at Georgina's stamina and began to doubt her own. Working in close proximity they established a mutual understanding, even intimacy, but an underlying reserve remained ready to ignite into hostility. Because of Dominic, Vanessa thought in puzzled conjecture, but that's illogical. She had no claim on him. One kiss . . . that's all.

Any break in the mad routine was rare, even for a decent meal, making the visit of Georgina's agent and publisher a precious breathing space. The morning was chilly but fine and, taking a flask of coffee, Vanessa and Fabian escaped like two furtive miscreants into the open.

"Absolute heaven." Vanessa pushed back her luxuriant hair and drew great quantities of oxygen into her lungs. "You'll be pleased to hear the masterpiece is in the last stages. Georgina may be finished but I can't keep up. Obviously, I merely *imagined* I was the perfect secretary." They'd had little time to talk, Fabian staying discreetly out of the way, and Vanessa was bursting for news of Dominic, his mysterious comings and goings and obscure comments a challenge. Where was he and why hadn't he visited? Was he being elusive because of Georgina's frenzy of creation?

Fabian seated himself sedately on the conveniently fallen tree-trunk. "We used to sit here years ago, all three of us. George always in the best place."

Vanessa asked: "Am I being too inquisitive?"

He poured the coffee, very delicately, not spilling a drop. "You are asking perfectly normal, healthy-minded questions but ... " seemingly at a loss for the correct words, he added, "some I can't answer."

"Because of company rules."

He made a boyish grimace: "They don't cover us, thank the Lord."

"But they cover Dominic." She offered it as a statement and Fabian nodded. "The old man's pretty rigid."

"A brute and a bully!"

"No. Just rigid. In contrast to my father, he gave Dominic everything he wanted . . . within reason naturally. Not that the idiot asked for much . . . sometimes he asked for something for us."

Vanessa sipped from her beaker. Everything he wanted but not everything he needed; no women; no loving cuddle: a cold, strict routine. She sighed and thought of her own childhood: a mother who drank to excess; a stepfather who sarcastically dampened her childish fancies; and later, a constant fight for Janie, fiercely protective, determined to help her young sister's ambitions. Dancing . . . which she did beautifully; riding, as one with her horse, extravagances won by Vanessa after much pleading and months of self-denial. Looking back now, Vanessa knew she had been a fool but she still felt she had done all she could to help Janie get over her ordeal and compensate a little for their lack of a mother.

Fabian said: "This is a vantage point for a wonderful view, but there are snags."

She stared across the low, retaining fence into the distance. As often, the hills were faintly misted, giving the beauty of the many hued heathers an unreality, as though the artist had run out of inspiration.

"A serpent in Eden," she said. "What snag?"

"This mist. When it hangs about it's a danger. A sudden stiff breeze and hey presto, landscape enveloped in minutes in a damp, impenetrable blanket. If ever you see it swirling, head straight for home in a hurry and never, ever, venture out of doors until visibility is clear."

Vanessa said, surprised by his

uncharacteristic depth of feeling: "Have you experienced being out in the mist?"

"Years ago. Dom and I were out all night searching for Joanna, my girlfriend. She was dead when we found her." His shoulders lifted in helpless regret. "An hour earlier, even half an hour, and we might have saved her. We were all very young. It took a search party to get us out and we were treated roughly I can tell you. We should have alerted them in the first place. I had a God-almighty tongue-lashing and the old man whisked Dom off home that very night. As if we hadn't been through enough . . . and finding Jo, face downwards . . . "

He shuddered and Vanessa said quickly: "It was natural . . . and courageous of you both to try and find her. I'm sorry, Fabian."

"As long as I've got the message over."

"You have."

Her imagination working overtime,

she capped the flask and stood up, brushing the few clinging leaves from her skirt and walking to the boundary to gaze at the view. The mist was barely visible, like all killers, something that crept up unawares. The picture of Dominic, straight-backed, eyes changing with his mood, sent a cold chill along her spine. Why did she have these premonitions? Was he in danger? Where was he? She asked the question again, not turning but willing an answer and, this time, Fabian answered, abruptly, angrily. "He's in Beirut risking his life for a blasted machine, and he'll kill me if he gets to know I've said so."

Two weeks later, very suddenly, the panic was over and, dazed by the anticlimax, Vanessa and Georgina exchanged exhausted glances as they slumped back in their chairs.

"We'll have to counteract this," said Georgina. "This awful feeling of being out on a limb gets more unbearable every time a baby goes out into the wicked world. So damned vulnerable, y'know. We'll have to throw a party, one to end all others, and if Dom doesn't come back in time I'll kill him."

Not a fortunate phrase, thought Vanessa, and inwardly sighed as she guessed who would shoulder the workload.

Georgina was saying: "Invite every single body you know, friend or foe. It's such fun to have a mixed crowd especially if they get at each other's throats." She laughed, the shrillness showing her highly strung state. "Oh dear God, Vanessa, do try to be co-operative. You've put on your po-face. Why do you disapprove . . . because I hope for a miserable few hairs flying?"

"Because," Vanessa said dampeningly, "I have very few people I can invite . . . friend or foe."

Georgina shrugged the statement off as nonsense. "Get on inviting anyway, you'll dig up a fair number when you think about it."

"To come to a party to end all parties

I possibly might." Vanessa spoke wryly. Little did she guess how true this was to be.

The event was fixed for the following weekend, such short notice sending everyone into frenzied action. Miraculously, Dominic arrived two days in advance, entering the hall to look around with raised eyebrows. "What goes?" he asked.

"The one who must be obeyed has ordered a party." Fabian seized the heaven-sent opportunity to cease dragging furniture about and Georgina, also deserting her task, swanned gracefully across the room to put her arms around Dominic's neck while she kissed him soundly on the lips. "Home on cue . . . just a bit before, so now you can help Fabian move the furniture and fix the lights. Had a good trip, darling?"

He counteracted with another question: "How's the book?"

"Finalised and approved. Another bestseller. Hence the party."

"Congratulations." He sounded weary rather than complimentary and she said sharply: "And you're coming, Dom, don't dare to tell me you aren't. Promise."

"No promise." He disentangled from her grip, his sudden slanting glance catching Vanessa's speculative regard: "Earning your daily bread?"

"Yes . . . now." She gave him a faint smile before turning to put the finishing touches to a massive array of flowers, all from the garden. He looked ill, she thought, and wished Georgina had more sensitivity. But Georgina was plying him with questions, most of which he skilfully side-tracked before moving to step on to the patio.

His need to get out was obvious but, even so, she ran after him. "Going up your precious hill . . . I'll come with you, I need a break."

"No." He used what Vanessa secretly dubbed his boss's tone. "Later perhaps. Now I'm going alone."

It seemed Georgina knew the tone

too. With ill grace she stood watching until he had crossed the lawn and let himself through the gate. After that the path was winding and he was no longer in sight.

"He's touchy," she said to her brother. "Do you know any more than I do?"

"No." Fabian spoke almost as curtly as Dominic. "Why don't you leave him alone. You know he hasn't a reliable aide and it must be hell trying to cope with a novice as well as a load of savages."

Vanessa fumbled and let several delicate blooms fall to the floor. She had read about the Lebanon and found the reports confusing. What had come through loud and clear was the lack of civilised organisation. Who was fighting whom! Israelis against Arabs. Syrians against everyone. There were names like dissidents, mercenaries, Druze militia, districts in Beirut such as Shi'ite Muslim, numerous revolutionary groups, several fronts and, of course, somewhere in the battle, Ayatollah Khomeini.

She sighed, feeling thoroughly ignorant and wondering how many other women felt the same or if Georgina and Fabian were wiser. She picked up the fallen flowers and, in sudden rebellion, pushed them into any available space. Displaying beauty seemed such a futile, pathetic occupation in the face of what was happening out there. Why didn't each country stick to their own boundaries!

At her shoulder, Fabian said: "Let's prolong the break and drink coffee on the patio while the sun is hot. Believe it or not, George has agreed to make it. Dom does have that affect on her at times and we all know he doesn't approve of you doing all the work. He's a stickler for the protocol, or haven't you noticed?"

She dragged her mind back to the present. "I've noticed," she said and wished passionately that she didn't notice so much about Dominic Russell.

4

DOMINIC had brought ten children back from Beirut. Unused to children, he'd found the responsibility exhausting even while marvelling at their astonishing resilience. Only one, a mere baby of three, had wept continuously for her mother; the others, aged between eight and eleven, had scampered through the long ordeal of officialdom, slept dreamlessly on any flat surface available, eaten ravenously and plagued the air-hostesses as well as scandalising many of the other passengers.

Towards the end of the journey, Dominic had given up trying to keep control, closed his eyes and ears to vitriolic comments and tried to hark back to his own childhood, finding no parallel. He had hated losing his father, while these children seemed blissfully unaware of their status as orphans. True most of them were returning to indulgent grandparents, a mixed blessing he'd never known, the paternal side long dead and the maternal apparently non-existent; three of them were doubled with a brother or a sister, two were fostered and the eleven-year-old had self-assurance far beyond his years.

Dominic stared at his beloved hills without seeing them. At eleven he'd still been heavily disciplined, not scared, but slightly in awe of the man who ruled his behaviour. He had learned very early that it was policy to adhere to regulations, much less hurtful than spending endless, lonely hours in isolation.

These children were not disciplined any more than young Pelham and they would have to face a tough world in the future. Poor little devils.

He eased his shoulders as if lifting a burden but he was still far from peace of mind. Not a simple matter to shrug off the massacre of thirty intelligent men and women, nor to erase the grief, endless questioning, barely concealed hostility of the relatives. He knew only too well that the workforce should have been evacuated, had tried to persuade those in charge to listen to reason but, dedicated, and with the end of the project in sight, they had appealed to his father, who had promptly, knowing little of the circumstances, given permission for them to stay.

Dominic's tight mouth twisted. The old man had accused him of going soft. Maybe he was. Sick to the soul he turned his back on the sight that no longer gave him pleasure. Instead he saw the mangled bodies under the wreckage of the razed factory and, inwardly, writhed for the human waste — all because of a priceless machine now buried deep underground in a fortified cellar. Let it stay there and rot, he thought. But the trouble was it wouldn't. Structured to outlive exterior erosion the diabolical monster would exist for a hundred years, always a threat to peace. Greedy men would fight and murder for the advanced technology, using it as a weapon and not for the purpose it had been constructed: advanced medical science on human brain abnormalities.

He thought again in wretched despair. Let it rot. I'll never go back. But he knew he would, if only to pay tribute to his dead colleagues. Johnny, undersized and brilliant, ever irritating with his habit of facetiousness. Other people he had come to like and admire: little five-foot Janice, bright-eyed, excited by the importance of the work she was doing, astonished at the brutality of everyday scenes, that religious war could break all commandments.

Her craving ambition had been to walk around Beirut, to see what was going on, to understand why the act of destruction was rife, why the Israelis wanted the land back, why the Arabs hung on. Whose land was it anyway? She had plied Dominic with questions, avid for information, draining him of everything he knew which, in some instances, was very sparse as it was difficult to keep ahead of the ever-changing situation.

Now she would no longer clamour for information, young face bright with interest. Nor would she ever see Beirut or any other foreign soil. Instead she had left grieving parents and a stunned boyfriend: *We were going to be married in the Spring.*

Spring! It was a season he might not see for himself.

He moved back to lean on the rail and felt it slacken, reminding him to instigate a repair before someone took a fall. There were other repairs to be done too, the greenhouse roof, tiles above the attic window loosened by a recent gale. Slowly he went down the path to halt when he could see the whole of the house, smug in the afternoon sunrays. *His* house, given to him by his real father, twenty-five years ago, before he went off, a gift to appease guilt. He was abroad now, somewhere where life was enjoyable, his visits to England growing fewer and fewer.

They were on the patio, Fabian to the rear, Georgina with her flowing mane and shapeless garment. And Vanessa, the girl who didn't know what life was all about, unaware and innocent. Or did one use the adjective 'ignorant' in these enlightened days. It was time she woke up. He couldn't bring the dead to life but he had other material to hand and a little indulgence would help him along.

At that time, under stress, Dominic didn't question why it had to be Vanessa who suffered with him. As far as women were concerned he was as ignorant himself.

Georgina walked to meet him, linking an arm as they crossed the smooth lawn, chattering about the coming party, trying to lift the shadow from his face. He knew and was grateful in a detached kind of way. Her character was familiar to him, not adding prestige to his general view of the 'weaker sex'.

No woman in his thirty-one years had ever given him what he really needed, simply a physical relationship to suit their needs but nothing else, no deep friendship, no shared interests, no . . . he hesitated over a word he shied from . . . love.

"We've stopped operations for today," Georgina said, then gaining no response added, her tone cajoling: "Sorry about the party, if you're feeling grim, but it's too late to cancel now. We've invited the world and his wife and it should be a riot. But Dom, please stay, if not for me, for Vanessa." As this insinuation fell on stony ground she tried again. "And your father refused the invite, so that's a consolation."

Flatly he said: "I don't see the reasoning, Georgina, not on either count."

"Stop being sticky. Surely, as things are . . . ?"

"He doesn't want to see me until more data has come through in any case. Useless discussing half-facts. I still don't see what difference his not coming makes."

She chose to ignore the bite in his tone: "He was ever adept at prolonging the agony."

With a muffled sound of impatience, Dominic shook his arm free: "And you were ever adept at mixing fantasy with reality."

She exclaimed, equally curt: "Reality to me is having you safe here, where you ought to be, not sweating over — " With a sigh she cut off the sentence. "Oh well, you'll do as you like, you always did. Sometimes you have the devil in you. I suppose you'll condescend to stay tonight, for the meal, at least? Vanessa's cooking up something."

"I'm staying." He paused with a foot on the stairs. "Where is she now?"

"Probably in the kitchen and she won't thank you if you intrude — she's already thrown Fabian out and he's the most amiable of creatures."

His tight mouth relaxed: "Thanks."

"Think nothing of biting my head off."

"Sorry."

She stretched up to kiss his cheek: "The king can do no wrong. Good luck, my darling."

Vanessa was struggling with a stubborn cork and was oblivious to his quiet tread. Curiously he stood and watched, wondering why she didn't use the steam opener fixed on the wall not a yard from her head. In the end he asked, with startling effect, and she swung round, the bottle slipping from her fingers and the loosened stopper releasing its final grip.

"Now look what you've made me do."

Usually women's logic irritated but now, surprisingly, he felt amused, more interested in her ruffled appearance than the wine oozing stickily around her shoeless feet. He wondered if it was customary to strip off in the kitchen, for it was obvious, Vanessa wore only a pretty nylon overall, matching the wide band tied around her head and failing completely to hide her femininity or constrain her luxuriant growth of hair. Under his frank survey her colour rose, highlighting the vivid blue of her eyes and the challenging set of her chin. She said smoulderingly: "Don't you know, Mr Russell, sir, that the domestic quarters are sacrosanct to the cook. I suppose you were one of those awful children who invaded the kitchen every five minutes?"

The barb hardly touched him; he had never invaded a kitchen in his life. He pointed out the cork dispenser and was rewarded by a furious glare and a quiver in the defiant reply: "I don't know what half the wretched gadgets are for. It's like working for a certain firm, you only know what you find out."

"As bad as that?" It was a disinterested comment. The world of machines and vicious warfare was, momentarily, pushed out of his mind, a hot, cross virago of a girl dominating the stage and separated from him by a pool of wine. He moved to pick up the bottle, automatically glancing at the label in an unconscious effort to control his raging emotions. "This is inferior."

"It's right for what I need."

He tried not to look at her and failed. "Vanessa . . . "

"Go away."

"I think I'd better before you stick to the floor. Do you need any help?"

"No . . . thank you . . . "

He knew she watched him go, felt her eyes on his back as if he had betrayed his need of a human touch, a weakness he had been taught to hide from childhood by a man made bitter by the desertion of a wife and brother. Dominic felt shattered, hearing again his uncle's anguished cries reverberating round the walls of the house that had become a bleak prison to a small boy.

In deference to Dominic's state of mind, Vanessa put on the same green dress and was far outshone by Georgina's flimsy, flaming robe that put Adrienne's former braless expedition in the shade. The meal was all right but not her best effort. Her expertise learned from Fabian over the last weeks had been set back by Dominic's unexpected reaction at the sight of her near-nakedness. She began to think he was an ordinary man under the frigid veneer and remembered clearly his jibe that all men were alike under the skin. She had better, she thought, lock her door when she went to bed.

As the pre-dinner cocktails and the plentiful wine took effect she watched him relax. Usually he was a selective drinker, refusing inferior wine and adamant about a refill when he had drank enough. Tonight he was drinking indiscriminately, his thin face growing flushed and, with the coffee, he accepted two generous brandies which, she mused, would add to his misery when he woke in the morning. Deeming it unnecessary to lock the door, she was in bed before the others and couldn't settle, listening for every footstep on the stairs.

Georgina had suggested they leave the men to talk and had wandered from the patio into the conservatory patting Dominic on the shoulder as she passed and giving the expected invitation.

He had nodded without looking up.

So what! They were lovers. They had lived together for a long time. Tonight he surely needed an outlet or was he too drunk to care!

Vanessa turned her face to the wall and lay tense, listening. She knew his step, lighter than Fabian's and his way of whistling softly as he passed. She heard Georgina's noisy passage and her brother's quieter one, but of Dominic there was no sign.

Had he gone off into the night as he had before, driving a powerful car in the state he was in ... or climbed to the plateau to fight his devils in the dark? What had happened in Beirut?

She was invading his privacy, Georgina-style, and might have turned back but for the faint light shining through the banister rails. No sound from below, she went on, bare feet soundless on the thick pile. The big hall, with its rearranged furniture, looked unfamiliar in the muted glow from the lamps and she moved slowly past the great fireplace, nervous now, her pulse racing, hoping that he wasn't there.

He was, in the small sitting-room, head in hands and shoulders, normally rigidly straight, bowed in despair.

"Dominic." She stood over him, near but not touching, still the reluctance in her to make intimate contact. She expected him to snap but he didn't, merely said wearily: "I'm in no fit mood to entertain polite company."

Taken by surprise, Vanessa asked: "Am I polite?"

He made a small, muffled sound: "Dear young Meredith, you never fail to amuse me."

"Or make you angry."

"I've never been angry with you."

She said in fierce indignation: "And

that's a thumping lie — you're either angry or sarcastic."

"Ouch," he exclaimed. "Spare me and accept apologies. I'll do better in future. Now tell me why you make a habit of parading half-dressed."

Trapped, she stammered: "I . . . came down for a book."

"Now who's lying?" He lifted his head and it was an effort, making him wince. "Never mind, it isn't important unless you make a permanent habit of it. Go back to bed."

"I want to help you to bed."

"My head is on a block, but I think I can still weave my own way. I noticed you didn't knock back more than one of Georgina's diabolical concoctions?"

"I saw what went into them."

"Paragon. Lend me a hand then, pity to waste a journey. Can you bring yourself to touch me?" At her silent rigidity he looked up, eyes narrowing as he surveyed her expression: "I see what you mean about my despicable cynicism." Taking her hand he held it for a moment in his, then he lodged it on his arm, adding abruptly: "You, young Meredith, are cold and that isn't sarcasm. I refer to your exterior. Now shall we go?"

Negotiating the stairs seemed not to present much of a problem, although he gripped the banister and allowed her supporting hand, but, once in his room, he made for the bed and slid thankfully along it, closing his eyes with a muted groan.

Bluntly down to earth, Vanessa asked if he felt sick and received an equally blunt negative followed by the starchy information that he was never sick.

"Lucky old you. Try to relax then, toes first and so on. It does help . . . oh . . . and stop clenching your hands."

"Yes, Miss. Yoga and all that stuff. I know all about it, so you can get tucked up and forget about me."

"Soda water helps."

"How do you know?"

"My mother was an alcoholic."

He said nothing, just sighed, and

Vanessa turned at the door, saying with feeling: "I could help if you weren't so ... " What he was didn't emerge. He ordered her out in his boss's voice, and she went, subdued and no longer sympathetic.

The next morning, Vanessa had two panic phone calls, the first from Adrienne who was swiftly reassured and the other from her sister Janie, passionate and tearful:

"He won't let me come to the party." It was a pathetic wail. "Honestly, Vanessa, my life is terrible. You've got to get me away from here. Now! Do something about me. Don't you care any longer? Why didn't you come home when you got the sack?"

Vanessa said, striving for patience: "You know why, I took this job."

"But you could have come home. I asked you to. I hate being a dogsbody, hate it. Hate it."

Vanessa had been just that for many years, far too long. A familiar bleakness settling over her spirits she schooled her voice to quiet firmness. "Calm down, Janie. Tell me sensibly what this is all about?"

"I've told you. He won't let me come. He says my place is at home looking after him. Why can't he manage just for once? He's a selfish pig. As if I couldn't have a few days off after all I've suffered. What shall I do? Make him let me come, Vanessa. Insist. Say you need me."

For some reason the words 'after all I've suffered' struck a sour note, making Vanessa's hand tighten over the receiver. In this war-torn world it was time individual suffering was put into perspective. She couldn't remember Janie suffering as Dominic was doing. In fact looking back, she recalled her sister revelling in the attention she received. Conscious of someone descending the stairs and wanting to cut short the conversation, Vanessa spoke more sharply than she intended. "You'll have to stand up to him, Janie, you aren't a child any more. I can't help you, so, for goodness sake, stop whining and try to fend for yourself." With Janie's sobs echoing in her ears, Vanessa put down the receiver. Was it because they were parted for the first time that she heard nothing but self-pity in the frenzied half-truths?

From behind, Dominic observed: "Not a ministering angel this morning? The little sister I assume and needing help that is not forthcoming?"

"I can't help."

Still pale but elegant in slacks and sweater, it was hard to remember him accepting her ministrations the night before. He asked: "What's the trouble?"

"She says my stepfather won't let her come to the party, but I imagine it's more a question of transport." The phone rang again and she picked up the handset.

"Dominic," demanded a voice she couldn't mistake and with a grimace she handed the receiver over to Dominic. "Mr Russell."

He detached himself from the wall and, as she walked away, she heard him say: "Right away?" and then after a pause: "Yes, sir." What a formal way of addressing his father. Vanessa wondered if she was mistaken in hearing a hint of satire and couldn't resist glancing back. Dominic was standing at one of the long windows and there was nothing about his straight back to give any clue to his feelings.

As if conscious of her regard he swung round and held her gaze. His eyes were dark, she noticed, a real give-away.

He asked abruptly: "What about your sister? If you want her to come I can pick her up on my way back. Just arrange a time and let me know."

5

IT was a radiant Janie who arrived late Friday evening. Not waiting for Dominic to open her door she leapt from the car and rushed into Vanessa's arms, hugging her fervently. "It's been a perfectly heavenly journey." Her voice was shrill with excitement. "The car is magnificent, simply flies, and we had supper at a really old-world inn, anything I wanted, wine too. I can't have it at home ... well you know ... Dominic's marvellous ... "

Vanessa let the incredibly immature speech flow over her, looking over Janie's head to catch the glint of amusement softening Dominic's face. Janie had that effect on men; they didn't realise she was turned twenty, that she relied on others to pave her way ... expected to be protected.

Janie was saying: "I'm going to have

a super time this weekend. You won't be all big-sisterish, will you? I can take care of myself now. Have had to since you left me." She released Vanessa and swung in an arc. "What a wonderful place . . . and the garden . . . so huge. Oh Vannie, aren't you lucky. If only I could stay here for ever."

Vanessa said flatly: "Come into the house and enthuse over that. Mr Russell doesn't want to lean on his car all night."

The girl's eyes widened: "Do you call him that?"

"No. But you should."

"He said I could call him Dominic."

There was no answer to that. Raising a shoulder in a slight gesture of defeat, Vanessa put an arm into Janie's and propelled her indoors hoping Mr Dominic Russell wasn't prepared to relieve his frustration at her expense.

Adrienne arrived on Saturday morning, glamorous but subdued, overawed, she confessed, by her bedroom, the size of the estate and, most of all, being in the same house as the boss.

"When the taxi turned in I yelled for him to stop and it was only his dirty look that made me come on."

"Idiot. I've told you before . . . "

"I know . . . that we're all on the same level. But it isn't true. You're on his level but I'm not. I'm scared stiff of making a boob."

Vanessa laughed and then sighed with pleasure. It was wonderful to see her ex-flatmate again, she was like a fresh breeze blowing away uncertainties. Still smiling, she teased: "As long as you wear a bra there won't be any boobs."

They sat in the window exchanging confidences and Vanessa was laughing at yet another of Adrienne's absurdities when Dominic erupted from the direction of the kitchen, slowing his step as he joined them. Eyes very blue on Vanessa's animated face, he said in exaggerated pathos: "Georgina is throwing plates. Help is needed."

Vanessa felt light-hearted, in party

mood: "And she managed to miss you."

"Don't sound so damned regretful." His attention veered to Adrienne's scarlet face: "Welcome Miss ... er ... Adrienne, isn't it?"

"Yes," Vanessa said severely, "and you scare her stiff. I've told her you aren't the boss here." It was a challenge and she knew it, meeting a sudden intense glance that set her resident intuition tingling, warning her that whatever he appeared on the surface, underneath he was a deeply disturbed man.

Nevertheless, he remained in good spirits and the party mood gripped as the guests began to arrive. Standing a few paces behind the hosts the three girls watched the motley crowd assemble, Vanessa ticking off the names on her list while Janie and Adrienne passed succinct comments on the women's attire. As the arrival thinned, Janie leapt forward to peer over Fabian's shoulder, her high-pitched tone laden with resentment.

"All this fabulous gear," she exclaimed. "I wish I could dress like these people. I'm deadly out of date, and so's Vanessa. That green dress is sick-making . . . and years old." She swung about to scowl at the offending garment. "Makes you look ninety."

Vanessa didn't feel ninety and she was in a reckless mood now that most of her duties were ended. Every invitation had been accepted, the hall looked magnificent and the dining-room a masterpiece with the snowy linen, flickering candles and delicately arranged flowers. Nothing, when arranging a function, must outshine the ladies — her stepfather's words — and she was grateful for all he had taught, despite his stringency. Looking back in growing tolerance, she began to understand his position better. His marriage must have caused him many bitter moments.

And Dominic's father! He, too, had made a bad bargain. Turning thoughtfully to the stairs, she found

Dominic at her side.

"Well done," he said. "Now the evening is all yours and the caterers take over. Don't let me see you doing a single chore."

She gave him a fleeting glance and wished she hadn't. In evening dress he stabbed even more deeply into her consciousness, and to feel anything more than compassion was a danger she wanted to avoid. He put a tentative hand under her elbow and she jerked away. "I'm going up to change . . . and Georgina's watching anyway."

"So what? I'm not offering to zip you up."

She thought his attitude to his mistress very strange and, contrarily, felt snubbed when he walked away, mingling easily with the guests.

What *did* she want, she wondered, then stopped as her name was called and he came back, feet taking the stairs lightly.

"You froze me out of what I intended to say . . . that you don't look ninety — impossible. You look exactly what you are."

She fell into the trap and could have hit him as her cheeks felt scorched. But she laughed, gaining instant approval, a swift finger flicking her chin: "I'll have that other kiss later."

"There wasn't one promised."

"Promise me now." His dark brows raised in teasing enquiry and she floundered.

"I don't . . . " And then: "I must change. I don't want to miss a single moment."

He opened the door for her. "You won't, I'll see to that."

A mad shopping spree while Dominic was with his father had resulted in an alarmingly raised overdraft but Vanessa refused to count the cost as she dressed, her body rather frighteningly responding to the soft touch of pure silk underwear and her hips automatically moving to the swirl of her skirt. Yielding to Georgina's superior know-how, present fashion had dominated and, fleetingly, Vanessa grimaced, knowing her sister would wail in envy. But the moment of guilt was forgotten at what the mirror revealed and Dominic's reaction became the main factor, her lips pursing as she recalled his former description. He could hardly fit her into a Gainsborough frame now.

Dominic's reaction wasn't encouraging. He watched her entrance, then went on talking to Tony Pelham, and Vanessa remembered Georgina's reference to his conservative tastes. But it didn't make any difference to how she felt. At least Vanessa told herself so and set out to enjoy as many partners as were available, another thing he appeared not to approve.

"Regular little glow-worm." He appeared from behind a pillar and rudely whisked her away from a wimpy young man who was earnestly trying to explain the intricacies of modern verse, the sudden hard grip, after one carelessly limp, shortening her breath.

"Do you have to manhandle me?" she asked.

The killing fingers slackened. "Vanessa, it's true isn't it?"

"What?" She preferred to concentrate on his chin, but surprise made her lift her head and he muttered: "No it isn't. You're just the same. Those eyes and that stupid nose."

"I don't know what you're talking about.

"It's of no consequence. I like you best looking ninety."

Concluding he was impossible, she said: "Whatever else isn't true, it's true that I'm ravenous. I can't remember lunch."

"You didn't stop for any." With an expert turn he directed their steps towards the dining-room: "I'm taking you in to supper and before you ask if Georgina minds, she is escorted by the literary crowd, whereas I know less than half of the people here. Also, your guests are happy with Fabian and Pelham so you can relax. This table here, a prime one, I know, but reserved for us."

Relax! Vanessa watched his casual stride and wished she could, then felt immediate irritation with herself. Fool. But why not? He would soon disappear again and this was a night to remember.

Dominic returned with champagne, a choice selection of food and the information that he had commissioned one of the waiters to refill as necessary.

Again, Vanessa thought, why not? She had worked hard to achieve near-perfection. It didn't occur to her then that she had done everything with Dominic in mind.

On this occasion it soon became obvious he meant to keep her glass filled. Vanessa played along, reckless after appreciating the first invigorating uplift. She was being pampered by a man who was, surely, the most eligible of the company, a man who made the others insipid. He gave her full attention, never once glancing up as outrageously clad, waggling-bottomed females teetered past their table.

And she firmly believed she could cope when the time called for tough action. It was to be many months before she accepted the real reason for his surprising interest.

Later, when Vanessa had unashamedly eaten to capacity, they danced, Dominic guiding her every step and his hand warmly possessive against her back. She wondered dreamily why close contact with him had once made her shiver. Why had she been so silly, for so long? Janie was carrying no trace of her traumatic experience, her childish snuggling into Fabian's arms a trifle embarrassing.

Tonight she was not going to worry about Janie, not about anyone. She was shedding her inhibitions, tasting the heady pleasure of being a woman with an attentive man. Closing her eyes she let the awareness of his body touch the fringe of her senses. She was not surprised he was a good dancer, that his decisive hold gave her confidence to attempt steps she had not done before. Dancing became a dreamy delight. He was strong and she was safe. Their cheeks touched and rested and she sighed.

The music stopped and he murmured softly: "Wake up sleeping beauty, the next dance isn't so smooth, it's an old-fashioned waltz."

He had read the programme. The band changed tempo and Vanessa was precipitated into teeming life, as exciting, if not more so, as the soporific relaxation of the waltz. Whirling through space she clung to him, laughing, and was still laughing when they collapsed, breathless, into a convenient chair.

She was sitting on his knee, his arm tightly around her. "Help." Gasping she tried to disengage and he kissed her, mouth firmly insistent. "Little witch." He raised his head. "The red hair means something after all."

Indignant, she exclaimed: "It isn't red," and fell silent as he laughed.

"Whatever colour, it's beautiful . . . and encouraging." He stood up, sliding her into the chair and left to fetch cooling drinks, leaving her to ponder over his meaning.

A minute later, Tony Pelham was at her elbow. A pale thin young man he seemed very unsure of himself and looked embarrassed when she teasingly enquired if he had deserted Adrienne.

"Well, no . . . you see . . . "

"There aren't any duty dances."

Vanessa thought he was about to stand on one leg and was relieved when he didn't. Comprehension dawned and she said: "You were commissioned."

"Well, yes, but I'd like to dance with you."

She took pity and stood up, wishing she hadn't as the room made a curtsey. Too much champagne or the mad whirl! Once on the floor she felt better although her partner made no attempt to offer guidance. As they circulated, he said: "We watched you dancing. Good to see the boss relax for once. He had a bad show."

"Are you his PA?"

"For a trial. I'm not in the same street as my predecessor."

"Why did he leave?"

Pelham missed a step and apologised unhappily: "I'm not allowed to talk shop. He'd sack me if he knew."

And the Russells were renowned for sacking employees. Vanessa had to know and repeated the question. "We won't talk any more . . . just answer that one thing." She felt she must hear the truth.

The band finished with a flourish, and they walked off the floor towards the lounge area.

"He was shot in the back."

The shine went out of the evening and she was coldly sober. She had sympathy for Pelham but her fear was for Dominic who had such an unreliable assistant.

Vanessa couldn't settle, had to breathe cooler air to steady her mind before facing Dominic as if nothing had happened, as if the terrified Tony

95

Pelham hadn't already committed an indiscretion and was likely to commit more. In danger he would be useless.

There was a crowd on the patio but few had ventured into the floodlit garden; the reason was obvious, for a mist was rising, hovering with ghostly fingers intertwined with trees and shrubs.

For a while, Vanessa sat in a secluded corner to watch, finding the phenomenon chillingly fascinating. Like a blanket, had been Fabian's description and it was apt except that the descent was icy, sucking all the intense heat from the powerful generators.

People began to move indoors and she heard Dominic's voice giving directions. She stood up and he saw her, long stride bringing him swiftly to her side: "There you are. Inside please, we'll have to check names."

"Surely no one is beyond the boundary."

"Let's hope not. But we can't risk not checking. 'Fraid it's going to be bedlam if we have to provide overnight accommodation. Fancy sharing a bed." Not waiting for a reply he pushed her through the open window. "Close every exit, there's a good girl, and then check on the women. Don't forget the cloakrooms."

Vanessa checked her own guests and had a shock. An uneasy Fabian told her that Adrienne, Janie and Tony Pelham had gone for a walk despite his efforts to dissuade them. The mist had certainly been distant at the time but . . . "

She turned from him and ran, jumping the patio steps and ignoring warning shouts. Her hand was on the gate when a band of steel gripped her wrist, wrenching it clear and swinging her back towards the house. His voice low with smouldering anger, Dominic said: "Indoors. If you set a foot outside again I'll wring your neck. Fabian told me your sister is missing and she'll be searched for by the right people, who know what they are doing. First we must discover how many others are out."

His hold was bruising and she instinctively struggled, fighting a losing battle for freedom. Ignominiously dragged into the hall, Dominic seemed ten feet tall as he towered angrily over her:

"One step outside . . . understand? Are you entirely without common sense."

"Janie . . . "

"We'll find her and the other two, and I'll wring their necks too. They were warned." Eyes dark he looked down at her, his tone less brusque as he added: "Help check, Vanessa. Don't panic. Fabian and I know every inch of the rise."

"Can't I go with you?"

"No."

It was final. He let go of her wrist and she cradled it under her arm, hating his mastery, wanting to kick and then stifling a sob of frustration at his sudden fleeting flash of amusement.

It had gone in a second and he said: "We're wasting time. Off you go."

She obeyed, her mood black, furious with him and ashamed at her own behaviour. It was no help to know he was right.

A search wasn't necessary, the three culprits appearing before Fabian and Dominic, with Sam the gardener, had time to leave. Dominic simply walked away in disgust, leaving Georgina to say all there was to say to the girls and it was when Vanessa returned to the dancing that she found Tony Pelham propping up a pillar, licking his wounds. Serve him right, she thought, then thought again. Poor Tony. He was no match for Dominic, and although he obviously admired his boss, he was not cut out for his present job. He'd been excellent as a personnel officer, she recalled, a pleasant, smiling young man with exactly the right approach to staff and clients alike. Pity he'd been promoted into a post capable of wrecking his career.

But it was not her business. Vanessa

nodded to the glass in Pelham's hand: "A refill?"

"Better not. It's brandy and I've had three. Can I get anything for you?"

Vanessa shook her head. She had sobered up once and she wanted to stay that way. The mist was dispersing under a mischievous breeze and taxis were due to arrive for the guests who were ready to be taken to the nearby hotel. She said with a smile: "If I were you I'd go on to soda water and have something to eat. Has Adrienne gone to bed already?"

He brightened: "I'll nip up and see. Room four on the front she said. I . . . er . . . hope you don't mind."

"She's a big girl."

He nodded: "Some girl too. I'm glad I was invited here, good of the boss to ask me. I'll cultivate a relationship, if you know what I mean, date her from the office." The animated expression faded, leaving him pale. "That is if I . . . " His voice faded away, attention narrowing across Vanessa's

shoulder. Hurriedly he finished. "I'm saying too much again . . . but it's only to you . . . I don't know why . . . "
He pushed himself from the post and swayed slightly. "Oh, hell . . . "

Reaching them, Dominic seemed about to ignore his subordinate but as he firmly directed Vanessa towards the dancing, he said curtly: "Don't get drunk. We're getting the first flight in the morning."

They were leaving on the first flight in the morning to a place where men got shot in the back . . .

They danced quietly, leaving the floor when the band changed tempo, and those still standing capered madly or merely stood on one spot and gyrated.

Vanessa was tired, the mental strain of keeping imagination at bay adding to physical stress. She thought Dominic was too: he lacked his usual dynamic energy and, uncharacteristically, when the last guest had left and the family gathered for a nightcap, he dropped into a chair and wrenched off his bow-tie, letting it dangle limply from his fingers.

Complacently, Georgina exclaimed: "My parties are always a success. Apart from one stupid incident everything was perfect. Your sister is very childish, Vanessa . . . and that friend of yours . . . "

Vanessa made no comment; it was the best way of dealing with her employer when she was bitching. Fabian opened his mouth as if to protest, but it was Dominic who, quite accurately, imitated a cat.

Georgina laughed: "You can shut up. It's been generally noticed that tonight wasn't your scene."

He raised an eyebrow: "Have I a scene? Tell me about it sometime. No, dear Georgina, whatever was noticed, I have thoroughly enjoyed your bestseller party and I think much of the praise goes to Vanessa."

Georgina hitched up her dress, showing an expanse of shapely leg. Her tone mocking, she said: "You have taken her under your wing . . . of course I asked you to, didn't I, dear Dominic?"

"I believe you did, in a roundabout fashion."

She had the grace to laugh, accepting defeat. "All right, you aggravating beast, what do you think of the dress?"

"Which dress?"

"You know very well which dress I mean. Vanessa's."

He swung his tie. "Obviously not your choice, my child. Give it to Georgina."

6

VANESSA was crying softly into her pillow when he came to her, and he was devastated. "Have *I* made you cry?"

Startled, she sat up and reached for a tissue, scrubbing her cheeks and eyes with unnecessary vigour. Crossly she said: "Yes and no. I don't know why you've come. Just go away."

He said wryly: "No welcome. I'll go when I'm ready and that's after you've told me why you are crying."

"I wouldn't if I could . . . and you dislike illogical women who cry for nothing."

"Maybe." He sounded uncertain, something so unusual that she dropped the shielding tissue to stare at him, ruffled and hesitant, his dressing-gown slung carelessly over silk, monogrammed pyjamas.

Why hadn't he gone to Georgina? She couldn't ask. She was glad he hadn't. She felt disorientated, not shocked, nor afraid, just not knowing how to cope with the situation. I'm stupid, she thought — at twenty-two, not knowing how to accept, to take what I want . . . to be loved — and by him.

And tomorrow he was going to where men got shot in the back.

As if perceptive to her dilemma he moved slowly to sit on the bed, and from the moment he kissed her she knew he was going to give her what she wanted, the experience of sex, and with him. His mouth sought her breast, a butterfly touch, and she sighed, appreciating the sensitivity and the cleanliness of his hair as it brushed her chin.

"Don't be afraid," he spoke gently.

She wasn't, marvelling at her own response, the pleasure of his hands on her body, the unexpected delicacy. She had thought of sex as brutal after Janie's ordeal, not this incredible feeling of being in another world, of floating out of herself with nothing of importance except the final possession. He had to hurt her and he did but it was fleeting, possessiveness in her too, the grasp of her hands on him, her obedient movement, so natural, so willing, so intensely involved.

Then it was over, the wonderful moment, leaving her breathless, still clinging, not wanting to lose his warmth. He moved her into his arms, stroking her damp hair.

"Go to sleep, dear little girl."

She was sleepy, lulled into fantasy, still clinging, reluctant to let him go. "Don't leave me, please, not yet." Passionately, she wanted to keep reality away. He would leave and that would be all; a seduction meant nothing to him, an experienced lover. She might never see him again.

A shot in the back!

With a stifled moan she burrowed into him. "Don't go, please don't go away to that awful place."

It was a mistake, an impertinent step

she shouldn't have taken, an intrusion into his liberty. She felt his coolness and had to struggle with tears, biting her lower lip hard as he put her aside, leaving her to a lonely misery surpassing anything she had ever felt before. Useless perhaps to whisper she was sorry but he responded, bending to kiss her nose: "Hush. Just go to sleep and be sensible. I must get some sleep too."

Yes, he had to catch a plane. Vanessa held back the tears until the door had closed and, although she listened hard, Dominic didn't whistle.

In the end he didn't go until later the next day. Feeling a trifle light-headed Vanessa went downstairs to find Georgina in a tearing fury and, after an hour of her own heart-searching, this added upheaval seemed too much. She went outside to breathe the cool morning air, staring at what she inwardly called Dominic's hill. He had escaped to the rise on the day he returned from Beirut. What had happened to give him that awful grey look of despair? Something even more terrible than Paxton being shot in the back?

The band round her chest was joined by a brick in her stomach. Why did he have to go back? How could the value of a machine be measured against a young life? If only he had a more reliable aide. If only . . .

A hand touched her shoulder and she started, flaring hope falling to lower depths as Fabian asked in dire sympathy: "Hangover, Vanessa?"

Perhaps that was it. Her spirit writhed feebly. By lunchtime she would feel better, had to be on form to cope with the hungry guests. What had happened last night would fall into perspective, a soft voice and touch leaving her consciousness.

Dominic was, after all, Georgina's mistress, his first love, probably one of many. Young Meredith was far down the list. She leaned her hot head against a pillar. Was it always like this after sex or was the heaviness a forerunner of another premonition?

Fabian was waiting patiently, one of his roles in life. Unable to keep the misery from her tone she said: "Whatever it is, I can't cope with a tantrum."

"Neither can I, not at the moment."

On a sigh, she said: "Shame Dominic isn't here to give her what she wants."

"Er . . . " he was embarrassed, "she's not interested in that when she isn't writing. Actually Dom is the whole trouble. The old man is here. He arrived at the crack of dawn, got Dom out of bed and they're cooped up in the office. It's upset all the arrangements. Can you imagine Uncle J. tolerating George's crowd when they turn up, or him sitting down to lunch with them. He's the most hide-bound bureaucrat alive."

"This isn't his house."

"No it isn't and it isn't George's either, nor mine. We take liberties."

Vanessa asked curiously: "Haven't

you ever wanted a house of your own?"

"I have a house of my own, a glorified cottage on the border of Wiltshire. Perhaps, one day . . . when I marry . . . " His fair skin suffused with embarrassed colour and she turned to contemplate her surroundings. Who? she wondered. Surely not Adrienne? It occurred to her that he had spent most of the evening with Janie, but the thought died away as the knowledge of Dominic still being in the house surfaced along with hope. Perhaps he wasn't going to the Lebanon after all. Maybe his father had decided the risk was too great.

Impulsively, she exclaimed: "Fabian, what happened in Beirut? Why did Dominic come back without finishing what had to be done? What went wrong?"

He said in a low voice: "Everything, in a way. The timing, for one thing, although that was unforeseeable. After allowing the factory to function for years the dissidents suddenly decided to blow it up. Not the Sheik's fault in this instance. Dom was with him at the time, negotiating entrance and the evacuation of the workforce. Everyone was killed. Dom had the lousy job of bringing ten orphaned kids back to England, and facing a multitude of shocked relatives who'd been assured of their sons' and daughters' safety."

Horrified at what his words conjured up, Vanessa stared bleakly into his now pale face. There was nothing she could say, nothing she could do to help and, in the end, she went inside to struggle with her accumulated knowledge.

Dominic was standing in the hall waiting for her and she wondered why he hadn't joined them on the patio, until she saw his expression and then her spirits plunged even lower.

No greeting, no warmth. They might never have had the most intimate of human relations. A curt request: "Come over to the window, Vanessa, I must talk to you in private."

What terrible crime had she

111

committed? Not what had happened between them? Not the destruction of a lovely, dreamy interlude for her to treasure. Please no, Dominic. She said defensively: "I've a load of chores waiting."

He moved his shoulders impatiently. "To hell with the chores, what I have to say is more important. And I've told you before, let Georgina take her share . . . and Jane, it's up to them to take a stint."

If the atmosphere hadn't been so tense she would have pointed out his chauvinistic attitude in not mentioning Fabian or himself. Surely nowadays . . . She obediently followed to the window and wished his back wasn't so taut.

"Is it Adrienne?"

"Not that simple."

"For goodness sake, you're making me nervous."

He withdrew his gaze from the view to appraise her, his jaw softening. "How d'you imagine I feel?"

"You're talking in riddles."

Reaching for her hand he looked frowningly at the bruises on her wrist. "Did I do this?"

"When you dragged me indoors."

"I didn't realise how fragile you were. Now I do . . . and, Vanessa . . . last night . . . were you prepared? Had you taken precautions?"

This was the last thing she had expected. Heat scorched her cheeks and prickled in her hair. Dear heaven, she had not given the matter any thought at the time, not at all. What an ignorant fool she was, naïve beyond forgiveness, intellectually a moron. There was no need for her to speak, her guilt was blatant, and the darkness of Dominic's eyes had deepened to near black. He had every right to be angry. In these enlightened days men didn't expect a girl to invite conception. And in Dominic's case . . .

Vanessa turned away, struggling with tears, shaking off the hand he put on her shoulder. "It's my problem," she managed thickly, "no need for you to worry."

"No need!" He let his fury show. "Talk sense, confound you. If there is a child, it's mine, no doubt about that. D'you think I'd turn my back? Shelve my responsibilities? Leave you to cope with a fatherless child? — " He broke off, then said in horror: "Are you crying?"

"No. I never cry . . . "

"Hmm," he said sceptically. "Well, don't. I don't mean to upset you, well not much, but you must admit the situation is tricky. If I don't — I may be away for a long time."

"Dominic, don't go. It isn't worth — "

"What I do is not your concern." The words were brutal but his tone was mild. "The object of this disjointed conversation is to provide you with security if the need arises. I'll fix arrangements with my father, and we'd better go and talk to him. He's leaving shortly and I have a plane to catch. All right?"

It was anything but all right. Vanessa felt devastated at his calm assumption and the idea of discussing their intimacy with a third person. Dear heaven, she thought hysterically, men are different, cold-blooded. I'd die rather than be so humiliated.

For a second time she shook off his tentative touch. "Go away, catch your plane and leave me alone. How can you expect me to talk to your father? *How can you?* I'm a human, not one of your precious, diabolical machines. What you suggest is humiliating, too delicate a situation to discuss. You're insensitive, hatefully, selfishly insensitive."

Which wasn't true. Vanessa wept bitter tears behind a locked bedroom door. She had done him an injustice, inserted cruel wording for the simple fact of understanding. And how could she expect him to understand? She was a one night stand and his back was overloaded. He had accepted the dismissal without a word, walking slowly away.

She found her limbs trembling, seeing in a single flash the anxiety in his give-away eyes. "You bitch," she said aloud, "you despicable bitch." But she couldn't have faced the suggested interview and he had no right to suggest such an ordeal.

Vanessa was arranging the table flowers when John Russell walked in on her and, as she turned, she recognised the likeness between him and Dominic in the straight, almost arrogant walk, the guarded expression and the immaculacy of his clothes. But this uncle-cum-father lacked the lurking humour behind the eyes and his voice was harshly intimidating.

Surveying her with cold indifference, John Russell said: "Might I have a word with you, Miss Meredith?"

Thankful she no longer had to call him sir, Vanessa carefully replaced the rose she was holding, wiped her fingers and, astonished at her own calm reception, suggested the small sitting-room.

Afterwards, she realised her every emotion had, in the last twenty-four hours, been expended to the full, making the presence of the man aptly nicknamed 'God' a mere pin-prick.

He was looking round the room. "I'm leaving shortly. How many guests did Dominic invite?"

"As far as I know, only one. Miss Vernon is hosting. The number is forty-eight."

The hard gaze came back to her face. "It's high time the Vernons retired to their own homes."

And me with them, Vanessa thought, then was caught off balance as he went on. "I must have a word with Dominic about the matter. If you find you are pregnant contact me immediately. You'll live here after you are married."

Reeling under the impact, Vanessa managed: "You can't dictate his life, there's no intention of marriage. We don't . . . we haven't . . . " Under his straight stare she lost track, feeling shattered.

"You should have thought of that before, both of you. His child, my grandson."

Vanessa had the hysterical inclination to laugh. The baby could be a girl ... what then? What nonsense they were talking. What baby? Not for one magic interlude. She couldn't be so unlucky. Or lucky. Anyway she could have an abortion.

Now she did laugh. It was as if a steely hand clamped her wrist. Murder, she thought. *He* would be shocked to his puritanical soul.

John Russell looked pointedly at his watch. "I must go. I have a meeting in London. Remember, Miss Meredith, make contact if the necessity arises."

Vanessa watched him leave. Like hell I will, she vowed.

Janie was waiting for her upstairs, had made herself comfortable on the bed and was lying spread-eagled, regardless of decorum. Hands behind her head she regarded Vanessa with the familiar wide-eyed innocence which meant she was about to ask for something.

"And what do you want?"

Janie pouted at the directness. "You do sound cross. I s'pose it's 'cos Dominic's gone. Everyone noticed how you stuck together, last night . . . smooching while you were dancing."

Vanessa swallowed a sharp reply: "Come to the point."

"All right." Janie sat up self-consciously, threw back her length of hair and blurted: "I want to stay. It's heavenly here, and Fabian wants me to. I want you to ask George if I can." Hurrying on at the ominous silence, she pleaded: "Do, please. It's selfish of you if you won't. I can help, y'know. I'm a better cook than you are and I can do the flowers and things . . . "

Stunned, Vanessa repeated: "Fabian?"

"Why not? He wants to marry me."

Vanessa stared numbly at the sister she had sheltered since they had become orphans, failed to see any recent sign of maturity and hoped this was one of Janie's flights of fancy. She would do a

Dominic, ignore what she didn't want to hear. Dominic! Her stomach curled with fear. She must not give way to one of her dreadful premonitions. She would not. Trying to keep her voice level, she asked: "Why not go to him then?"

"She just laughs at him. He says you can cope. He says — "

Vanessa said sharply: "I can *not* interfere. You all seem to forget I only work here. I'm a paid employee and I want to remain that way." Walking to the window she flung it wide open, welcoming the rush of cold air. She was two years older than Janie, in some ways just as gauche, and she was suddenly afraid. Too many things had happened in too short a time and it was she, Vanessa, who needed a shoulder to lean on now.

The expected tantrum came and made no impact. Vanessa knew what she was off by heart. Selfish . . . and she had called him that . . . hard, uncaring. Vanessa gripped the sill. Fool that she was, she had fallen in love with a man who would retreat from the knowledge with distaste, who already had a mistress and had claimed another under the same roof — in the adjoining room.

How did this align with the narrowness of his code?

In the end, for the sake of peace, Vanessa went in search of Georgina, finding her in the kitchen, still fuming over Dominic's desertion. Knowing her quest was doomed from the start, Vanessa asked bluntly if Janie could stay and helped herself to a coffee under a keenly assessing eye.

"No she can't, and you aren't expecting me to agree, so why ask?" Receiving no reply, Georgina exclaimed: "Lord above, you do look a wreck. If you will open your door to Dominic what d'you expect? Did the crazy fool go the whole way? He's dynamite when he gets the bit between his teeth."

Which was not exactly how Vanessa would have described the gentle initiation. But Georgina's attack was another shock even though her probing could only be assumption. Swallowing the too hot coffee, Vanessa headed for the door feeling that if she didn't escape she would throw as wild a tantrum as Janie.

"Wait a minute." The words came suddenly. "Stand still. Look at me. Oh yes, darling, you're perfect. My next heroine *in toto*. All sensitivity and looking like a virgin. My hero'll fall flat for you and probably end up wringing your delicate little neck."

Which was what Dominic was likely to do, Vanessa thought wearily.

7

BY four o'clock all the guests had drifted away with the exception of Janie, whom Vanessa found sobbing uncontrollably beside a half-packed suitcase. Sitting down, Vanessa said quietly: "Janie, you said Fabian wants to marry you. Has he actually told you so?"

"No, but he will, I know he will."

"Has it occurred to you that if he saw you now, acting like a ten-year-old, he might not be so interested? You look a mess."

Always resentful of criticism, Janie flung back: "So do you."

Vanessa smiled wryly. "I know. I'm dog-tired, and you making this fuss doesn't help."

"You just don't understand how I feel . . . everyone against me, sending me home. All I want is kindness and understanding. Why have you turned against me? You always used to help. I'm sure if you really tried, Georgina would give way."

Vanessa raised a helpless shoulder and thought longingly of the small plateau halfway up the rise. A retreat. Had Dominic felt that way about the idyllic spot? She imagined him as he had come across her, hiding anger, too polite to throw her off his special place. He had wanted to; she'd sensed his frustration as he sat beside her, the tense stiffness of his body, the dark shadows in his eyes. She sighed and knew she was sighing too often and would go on doing so. Growing knowledge of a difficult man was bringing her no happiness.

Janie shrilled suddenly: "You aren't listening. You don't care any more — I'm just a nuisance to be got rid of, sent back to slave my days away." Pleading always came after aggression. "All I want is to be happy. I'll work like mad here, do anything I'm asked. And Fabian will marry me, really he will.

The silly man thinks I'm too young and virginal even though I told him I want him to be the first."

From the hysterical outcry, Vanessa seized on the salient point: "But you aren't a virgin."

"Yes I am." Janie turned a guilty shoulder and tugged at the neck of her sweater. "I wasn't raped. The beast did foul things to me . . . "

"But the doctor said — "

"You weren't there when he examined me. You were too busy wresting the gin bottle from mother." Janie shot a swift glance at Vanessa's white face, adding defiantly: "Anyway, I didn't know what rape really was and it sounded more dramatic than assault when I told the girls at school . . . "

Janie went on with the justification and Vanessa closed off her mind. She didn't want to hear any more, couldn't survive more shock. Battering her wincing sensibilities was the realisation of four years of unnecessary self-denial and grinding hostility against the brutality of sex.

She had to get away before she broke down, her parting words huskily intense: "The taxi will be here at five o'clock. If you aren't ready, Georgina will throw you out."

The big, rambling house was very quiet. Georgina had shut herself in the conservatory saying she wanted to be alone and Fabian having completed his own literary chores, asked Vanessa to go for a walk.

As they rounded the house towards the open fields, he said with unusual curtness: "I believe we've done the right thing, sending Janie home. She is so very young."

"For a twenty-year-old, yes." Vanessa spoke bleakly: "My fault entirely. I shielded her too well. Your prosaic friend considers her juvenile. He's right."

Fabian said gently: "Such bitterness isn't like you. Is it Dominic? He's difficult to understand sometimes. What has he done to you?" He slanted a sideways glance as she made no reply: "You're in love with him, not an enviable state of mind at this particular time. But there's nothing you can do; he's his own master and a tough one at that. He'll go his own way."

"Or his father's."

The reply was faintly reproachful. "Most people get that impression but, in truth, Dom is the stronger character. He was reared tough and, as sometimes happens, overtook his master. Don't get the wrong idea, Vanessa. Dom is the backbone of the company, fighting for its survival, defeating massive competition and thwarting takeover bids by pushing up remuneration to the shareholders. What's more, he has an affinity with the robots . . . a great pity . . . it means he can tell at a glance what the workforce take weeks to learn."

"So he has to risk his life for them."

"The occasion arises but not too often. All countries aren't warring. The job he's on now is tricky because it's unique. But don't worry. Dom can take care of himself. He doesn't rush in, waits for the right time. He is already acquainted with the people he's dealing with."

They reached a stile and Vanessa leaned across the bar. More pieces to the jigsaw, she thought, and wasn't much comforted. If one man could get shot in the back . . .

It was too cold to sit, so they turned back. "Does Dominic communicate?" Vanessa asked.

"He has a hot line to his father but Dom often maddens him by dropping off contact. I'm afraid it may be weeks before we hear anything."

"Where does Dominic stay?"

"In an hotel outside the zone, but mainly with friends in Cyprus. He's probably sunning himself at this very moment."

He was trying to be kind but his tone lacked conviction. He *was* kind, a man in a million, but Vanessa doubted he could manage Janie.

The conversation switched to Georgina's new book, Fabian of the opinion the idea would fizzle out. "She's never written a romance in her life," he said. "If this novel materialises it'll be a cynical caricature of facts."

Vanessa, remembering a certain conversation, said nothing. She firmly believed that neither Georgina nor Dominic knew what love was.

A few days later, Vanessa woke to find she wasn't pregnant and, for several hours, relief and disappointment struggled for priority. Then, according to the rule, she telephoned John Russell, replacing the receiver a trifle abruptly as the harsh voice uttered a curt acknowledgement, adding that his son would be immediately notified.

No emotion whatsoever. She wandered aimlessly from room to room. Fabian was busy with his favourite, delightful characters and Georgina didn't, as yet, require attendance. It was too cold to go out, windy and wet, snow threatening. She longed to climb the rise to the plateau, longed for news of Dominic. Restlessly she climbed the stairs, bypassed her own room and went into his. It was as before, scrupulously tidy, unlived in, the photograph, with its flamboyant message, taking pride of place on the chest. The room was cold and she walked slowly to close the window, pausing to appreciate the view that, even in winter, held soothing beauty, the boundary fence just visible in the frosty air.

She went downstairs, took the second extension in the small sitting-room and rang Adrienne, breaking company rules. Adrienne's first words were: "Tony's back. Oh hell you'll get me the sack. I'll ring you at six. I was going to anyway."

At six, Vanessa exclaimed in dire urgency: "Is it all over, a success?"

"I don't think so. The boss, 'God', is thunderous and Tony won't say much. Reading between the lines I think he's made another boob, mislaid some vital equipment or papers or something. He's having an awful time and it just isn't fair. Why should he have to do what he hates? It's diabolical of the boss to make him go again."

This was the other side of the coin but Vanessa was no longer sorry for Tony Pelham, she ached for Dominic's frustration instead.

Adrienne babbled on: "I do know it's a flying visit — ha! a pun . . . Actually, Tony would back out if he could, but he's under contract like we all are and the firm pays terrifically well. I'll never, ever leave. But it's different for him, Tony, I mean. He's strange, not himself at all. D'you think he ought to go back?"

Vanessa had no opinion. When she could insert a word, she suggested a lunchtime meeting: "I want to unload."

The date had to be put off and the onloading took a different form. In the interim, Georgina's so-called romance demanded constant attention and, inevitably, each day ended with an exchange of conflicting opinion.

She had based the heroine on Vanessa and the result was not flattering nor, in any way, the truth. It was not romance being written, but near pornographic material. The bedroom scenes were explicit and the hero a skilfully worded facsimile of Dominic. Georgina's possessiveness of him was manifold in every word, she seemed to gain no relief in conveying her feelings to paper, and lost weight, making her frighteningly fragile.

Or was she as worried over his safety as Vanessa?

Vanessa stopped protesting and humoured her volatile employer's problems while growing more and more anxious over her own. Under the circumstances it was impossible to talk to Fabian, a disloyalty to Dominic, but with Adrienne it would be different . . . woman to woman.

The long-awaited chance came several days later owing to a visit from

Georgina's agent, Jim Fletcher, a short, exuberant man with an abundance of ginger hair, an over-appreciation of pretty girls and a bottom-patting habit. Despite this, Vanessa could have kissed him, allowing the familiarity stoically and then, after writing a note of explanation, snatched up what was needed and fled.

At six o'clock she was sitting opposite Adrienne, sipping insipid tea and putting aside a plate of sickly cakes.

"I've no news so you can talk first. You look as if you need to . . . are you starving yourself?"

"My appetite is terrific, but not for gooey cakes. I can be sick without."

Adrienne's cup went down with a clatter, spilling the liquid. Eyes enormous, she exclaimed: "Don't tell me you've joined the club, you of all people. Jumping grandmother!" She blinked in disbelief. "I just can't believe it, and after the lectures you dished out to me." Suddenly comprehending, she leaned forward, forgetting the spilled tea and soaking her sleeve: "Oh damn and to blazes!" But at that moment, the damage was of secondary importance. "The boss, that devil Dominic Russell. After the party . . . he bulldozed you . . . "

"No."

"You were willing?"

"Yes."

Unsure of her ground, Adrienne shifted uncomfortably. She said gruffly: "I can't blame you. No girl in her right mind'd kick him out of bed. But he's an experienced fella, he wouldn't — "

Vanessa interrupted bleakly: "He didn't know I hadn't taken precautions."

Adrienne's mouth opened and closed in stunned condemnation. "Well, in that case you asked for all you've got . . . and landed him in the soup. He — "

Vanessa cut in again: "Dominic said about everything, so save the sermon. What I'm asking is for advice. You said your foster was always having babies. What do I do first?"

"Go see a doctor or visit a clinic

. . . but not first. First you hand over some responsibility to the great lover . . . or is it to be an abortion?"

"No. And I'm not telling Dominic. I can't. I told him I was all right. I thought I was . . . but the next time . . . well, I went to see the village doctor and the result of the test was positive. So you see I'm on my own now."

Adrienne said with stark impatience: "All I see is a raving lunatic. You can't 'not tell him', you idiot. He has a right to know and, whatever I think of him, he isn't the kind to shelve responsibility. He might possibly wring your ruddy neck though."

A distinct possibility. Vanessa smiled without much humour. She was determined that she would not put him to disadvantage, force him into marriage and, the way she was feeling in this primary stage of pregnancy, she knew she was in no fit state to fight for independence, not against the father and the son. *His* grandson, that hard old tyrant. Whatever the baby was, John Russell was having no hand in the rearing.

"Now what's going on in that tiny mind?" Adrienne asked. "Honestly, Vanessa, you'd be crazy to try and manage alone. Where would you live, for a start, and what about money? At least you could accept financial help."

"No. He won't know where I am . . ." Vanessa stopped, appalled at her own attitude. Of course, she couldn't afford to exist, let alone bring up a child; not as he would want his child to be brought up. But why did she care what he wanted? The thought of the baby had horrified him and he would only marry her because his father insisted.

Checking a growing tendency to weep she grabbed her cup, shuddering at the cold tea. Everything tasted different, beverages were revolting. Tears dampening her lashes she mumbled forlornly: "I'm in a mess. I feel a mess. I can't sort out the best thing to do."

Adrienne said flatly: "Lord save me from the trials of pregnancy. You feel like that, my dear imbecile, because of how you are. The Foster always wept for at least six weeks. Then she had fancies for unusual things, like prawns and tins of pineapple. Once I watched her eat a whole cucumber and, on one occasion, she ate all our lamb chops and left us with the vegetables." Her piquant face creased into laughter. "That's better, have a good howl."

"I'm not howling, I'm laughing. You must be the world's biggest liar."

"No lies, just exaggerations. What d'you fancy apart from a gun?"

Vanessa sobered and sighed: "He's in the danger zone. Don't let's talk about guns."

"Tony, too."

They stared bleakly at each other.

"It must have been like this during the war," Adrienne said, "not knowing if your man would come back. Why in hell do men fight? Why do we women care?"

"Evolution." Vanessa looked at her watch. "I'll have to go or I'll miss the last train. We only have two a day to the local station."

"And how do you get from there?"

"Walk."

"In the dark . . . a bit dodgy."

Vanessa thought so too when she got off the train to find a long country lane ahead. A by-road and a short-cut, it was rarely used except for cattle and this was very obvious as she picked her way between water-filled ruts and slippery substances.

Her thoughts fully occupied by the parting advice of the girl, who, through living rough, was more worldly wise than she was, Vanessa was unaware of the shadow at her heels.

Unload on him and let him take over. He's tough and money is no object. For Pete's sake, Vanessa, you aren't scared of him . . . you can't be . . . he's made love to you.

Yes he had made love to her and seemed a different man from the

138

one she had first met at a searing interview. The problem was, in her present predicament, she couldn't make up her mind which one he would be when she broke the news.

Always providing he came back from the crazy war-torn country where hostages were taken without discrimination.

Her foot slid into a wet patch and, at the same moment, she became aware of the furtive follower. Heart somersaulting, she fought to keep her balance and slipped further, sitting down with a spine-shaking thud on the filthy road.

Stark common sense knocked into her, Vanessa realised what an impulsive fool she was. She should have telephoned Fabian from the station. He would have picked her up and she would, by now, be warm and safe in bed.

How Dominic would despise her stupidity.

Why did she always think of Dominic's reaction?

The thing pounced, a frightening

shadow of arms and legs in the dark. A scream strangled in her throat and she struck out, horrified to find her fingers entangled in matted hair. A monster. For a moment, Dominic was there, his tone amused. Silly idiot . . . idiot . . . idiot . . .

Ice touched her cheek. She was hallucinating . . . a premonition. *Would* he be amused?

The coldness began to explore, bringing her to surging life.

"Get off. Get *off.*"

The situation had worsened, wetness rapidly forming ice. Trying to stand up became impossible. She was trapped, in choking blackness, unable to breathe. Dominic. Dominic.

Her mind cleared and she stared with amazement at the moon-illuminated surroundings. Well-trimmed hedges, leafless trees, the lane ahead glinting and white were all nearer to the house than seemed possible. The shadow had retreated, was lying at the side of the lane, panting, whimpering. A dog, pathetically bedraggled and bloodstained.

"Dear heaven," Vanessa said aloud, and felt foolish as she made another valiant effort to get up, this time keeping a foothold as she shuffled precariously to the verge. One should never touch an injured animal, she'd been told, and she didn't. But she leaned down to murmur a few soothing words knowing that the animal, if violent, would have savaged her while she was down.

"Poor old fellow. Come on I'll take you home." She took it for granted that it belonged to the farmer. Caught in a trap, no doubt, or run over. Against better judgement she fumbled for its collar . . . and found none.

And it wasn't a dog, it was a fox, barely emerged from the cub state.

8

VANESSA spent the next few days smiling grimly at the old, old adage. Life goes on. But in what a fashion: the usual round of flowers, meals, tidying after Fabian and, the most wearying of all, coping with Georgina. Vanessa had given up softening the lurid scenes in the book. They no longer offended her or made her feel sick. She didn't care. She felt light-headed, divorced from reality, even the daily visits to the fox-cub were a zombie attendance, its incredible show of affection barely registering.

It would leave eventually, was free to go, the injuries received healing rapidly in the warm shelter of the out-house.

Fabian accompanied her on one of these visits, making little reference to the fox but, as they re-entered the house, he asked Vanessa to go up to the attic with him.

"There's something I want to show you."

The attic was his holy of holies, sacrosanct, and she was intrigued to be admitted, expecting the utter chaos he was apt to create wherever he worked. But the large room was bare and pristine, lit by six large dormer windows and only one end showing any sign of use. Here were several easels, many paint-boards, palettes and, facing them, one large portrait.

"Do I really look like that?"

"Love has many faces."

Vanessa didn't ask him what he meant, she said instead: "Did you paint the portrait of Georgina, the one in Dominic's room?"

"Yes. But Georgina wasn't in love, has never been in love, except with her imaginary heroes."

Vanessa said slowly: "You've flattered me. It's kind of you, but I don't *feel* I look as you have painted me. It's beautiful."

He had dressed her in the colours she favoured, soft green, a warm touch of sun lighting her hair, a yellow flower in her hand. A buttercup.

Fabian said: "It's how others see you. Dominic liked it. All spring and summer, was his verdict. How Vanessa should be. Autumn perhaps but never winter." He didn't tell her that Dominic had added harshly: "Cover it up. Why did you show it to me? You know I'm not interested enough to give proper appreciation."

Fabian covered the portrait now, turning the easel to the wall. "One day I'll give it to you, both of you, at the right time."

Vanessa asked, changing the subject: "May I see some of your other work?" She wouldn't ask if he had painted Dominic, though curious to know, but when he eventually uncovered the likeness she stared without comment, unsure whether she liked the candid portrayal.

Fabian said with a smile: "Not

good I'm afraid. Dominic is practically impossible as a subject. I don't really see him like that; my brush betrayed me." He covered the easel and drew out another canvas. "This is better, he was caught unawares by my camera and I painted from that. Not satisfactory but better than trying to read his mood from life."

It was of a younger Dominic, casually dressed, dark hair ruffled and laughter softening his face. Ten years younger perhaps, but the same lean look of physical fitness. And, behind him, his beloved hills, sleeping, the sun riding high and throwing no shadows.

Fabian covered the canvas: "He was about twenty-two then, home for the long vacation, the last time he stayed the whole time. Uncle J. was abroad for six months."

The title sounded strange and Vanessa asked: "Is Mr Russell your uncle?"

"Not in the true sense. We're related along the way but very distant. As children we called him Uncle, George and I, even Dominic when the old man was out of hearing. It takes time to change a title, easier perhaps because of the physical similarity. But Dom's real father and Uncle John weren't alike in any other way. Jeff Russell would have dragged Dominic from pillar to post, no decent schooling or university. Jeff spent his money on women, not on his son."

"Didn't you like him?"

"Oh, one had to like him — he was a charmer, played games with us whenever he turned up. But he never married . . . not even John's wife after the divorce. Poor Aunt, she tried to come back but was turned from the house. Can't say I blame the old man . . . would any man have a wife back who'd run out on him."

Vanessa found no sincere reply and went to lean on the sill where the window faced the hills. But she was restless and the view made no impact. Where was Dominic, she wondered.

From her shoulder, Fabian said: "I'm

running George into town tomorrow. How about joining us — we could all do with a break. Perhaps you and Adrienne can have lunch together and I . . . well, I'll pay Janie a visit."

He had not mentioned Janie since her tearful departure and there was a depth to his voice that made Vanessa change her mind about refusing the offer. Anything was better than another long day moping about this house, which had suddenly lost all charm.

Adrienne was not free for lunch and Vanessa went to their usual venue in no better spirits. A browse round the stores had merely served to depress her more and her buying enthusiasm was nil, resulting only in a silk scarf intended for someone's Christmas present and a brooch she knew her sister would like.

In a restaurant full of chattering people, she felt very much alone, her mind temporarily ceasing the see-saw emotions swinging from Dominic to her own situation. She had meant to go into the baby departments, she still could, but she knew the inclination had faded. Adrienne, in her old world wisdom, had been so right when, on their way to the station, she repeated the necessity of unloading onto Dominic. "A pregnant woman," she'd said, "needs a shoulder to cry on."

The smart little waitress asked for the second time: "D'you mind sharing the table with a man who says he knows you?"

Vanessa hadn't lived in London without meeting this claim before and discrediting it but, glancing round, she saw there was very little space elsewhere and knew it would be childish to refuse.

The man was youngish, pin-striped and not unhandsome. He dropped his coat and umbrella to the floor and smiled as he sat down. "I really do know you, Vanessa Meredith. I also lunch here sometimes with Adrienne. I can see you don't remember me."

She didn't, not even when he

introduced himself as Guy Middletone and, after ordering a steak, said: "Like you I was booted out of the Russell organisation but they didn't find me another job, the damned despots. All I made was one small slip but trying to justify myself made no impact. However ... " The wine arrived and, after Vanessa had shaken her head, he poured out his own. " ... however I fell on my feet. I'm a freelance and reporters have many ways of getting back." He took a generous amount from his glass. "And, anyway, I have lots of lovely free time and no blasted rules. That place was like prison. Who d'they think they are, a couple of gods? Good nickname for 'em, don't you think?"

Her backbone sounding a warning, Vanessa pushed her cold salad around the plate and, when the steak he had ordered arrived, she asked the waitress for coffee.

Not seemingly daunted by her lack of sympathy, Guy Middletone went on: "I've a good nose and the grapevine is ashake. Rumour has it there's dirty work at the crossroads. Woman trouble, computer leaks, employees getting murdered in that godforsaken hole out East. The Lebanon, you know? There's been trouble abroad before. It's time the Russells cut their losses and concentrated on their own country. What d'you think?"

Vanessa couldn't say what she thought. This man was without principles, despite his pleasant façade. Underneath his rapidly slurring words there was venom. He was a man with a grievance, his own shortcomings and lack of loyalty something he refused to recognise.

Trying to keep her tone impersonal she asked: "What can you do? Isn't the firm impregnable?"

"Dear girl, nothing and no one is impregnable in my job. A few more facts and a whiff of confirmation and I sell to the highest bidder. I can see the headlines: 'Russell Foundation employees murdered in a well-known trouble spot! Enquiry into why the workforce wasn't pulled out'." He drained the wine and refilled the glass. "Sure you won't have a drop? Keeps out the cold y'know."

Nothing would have dispersed the cold inside Vanessa, not even the good, hot coffee. There was enough truth in his statements to be frightening. How much responsibility of the massacre could be laid on Dominic's shoulders?

It wasn't difficult for her to get away and, once out in the street, she knew what she had to do. She flagged a cruising taxi and went to see John Russell.

The house was as she'd imagined, square, shuttered and as stolid as the reception she received from the butler who opened the massive door. The sound of bolts being withdrawn was in keeping.

"Mr Russell is at lunch," was the answer to her request. "If you'd care to step inside I'll ask if he will see you. What name shall I say?"

He was back before she had time

to thoroughly assess the surroundings, the overall impression that the big, sparsely furnished hall was as cold as its owner.

Shown into a dauntingly impersonal drawingroom, Vanessa crossed at once to the fire, asking over her shoulder: "May I have some coffee, I'm very cold."

"Certainly, Miss Meredith. Cream or milk?"

"Just black and strong."

"Mr Russell had ordered it. He's taking his in here."

Left alone, Vanessa appeased her curiosity. The room was in the front of the house, heavily curtained and expertly sound-proofed. Large enough to accommodate two suites, it also contained items of solid oak furniture, all sedately aligned and showing no sign of permanent use. The carpet, wallpaper and curtains were all of the same shade of indeterminate grey, giving the room a sombre look, in no way assisting the solitary fire to add warmth.

If the rest of the house was similar, Vanessa didn't blame Dominic for escaping as often as he could. It was a sobering thought that he'd spent a great deal of his life here.

John Russell came in with a table napkin still in his hand. He suggested she should sit down and suspended conversation until the butler had poured coffee and a generous measure of cognac into two heavy cut-glass goblets. Then he sat down himself and waited. There was no doubt that, besides being a despot, he was a perfect gentleman.

Making no apology for interrupting his lunch, Vanessa told him, simply and accurately, about Guy Middletone and his open threats then, in turn, waited, watching him over the rim of her glass. His eyes were grey, she noticed, his facial expression guarded; his jaw, like Dominic's, was firmly authoritative but, unlike that of his adopted son, John Russell's mouth lacked the hovering humour lifting the corners of his mouth. Perhaps, she thought, this characteristic came from the other twin and she wished she could meet him.

The brandy and the fire were beginning to warm her and she sat more comfortably in the fireside chair, inwardly marvelling at her own self-possession. It occurred to her she need never have feared this man, that he carried his burdens heavily and his hard front was a protective shield. A man who rode himself too hard. A man who denied himself a woman.

John Russell said, the harsh strain noticeably softened: "I appreciate your concern, Vanessa. Middletone is a questionable character and should not have been employed. Unfortunately, both Dominic and I happened to be absent when he was interviewed and his dossier escaped our scrutiny. Eventually we dismissed him because he was a troublemaker, undermining the staff and quite deliberately breaking the rules of contract. By now you know how important it is for us to have trustworthy employees." He paused to sip from his glass then put it aside unfinished. "The loss of workforce was entirely my fault, I overruled Dominic and I should have known better. It was unfortunate that his efforts to get the factory cleared were strongly opposed by the workforce themselves, who needed less than a week to complete their contract. As for Paxton, he signed his own death warrant ... ignoring the order to halt and running across open ground. Dominic can hardly be blamed for another man's panic."

Vanessa looked down at her clenched hands. "And Dominic now?" she asked.

"I don't know where he is. Sometimes he cuts off communication, either through sheer defiance or for the sake of caution."

"Or the communication could have been stopped."

He made no immediate reply but said eventually: "We cannot be sure at this stage. Dominic's base is in Cyprus. He may be taking a break."

"But surely, if he's in Cyprus and safe, he'd let you know?"

"Not necessarily."

Not realising the significance of this, Vanessa felt her colour rise. "He couldn't be so inconsiderate. He must guess how worried we all are." A too candid observation making her cheeks burn more fiercely. She wondered why Mr John Russell was being so frank with her and was still astonished he had called her Vanessa. He was certainly offering a different side of himself. Realising they were at stalemate, she asked: "What can be done about Guy Middletone?"

"He poses no problem at all. He has a criminal record and I rather think the Russell organisation can withstand a few brickbats."

9

ON the journey home, Vanessa went over and over the conversation and could find no comfort. She simply refused to believe Dominic would cease communication for a whim, although it was a disquieting thought that he had no responsibility towards her, not knowing she was carrying his child. Uncomfortably, she reviewed John Russell's parting words: "Take more care of yourself." Now why had he said that? He couldn't possibly know the pregnancy had been confirmed. No one knew but Adrienne.

More disquieting news came when Fabian announced, with unusual defiance, that he had invited Janie to stay for a day or two at the weekend. Vanessa was disturbed but she closed her ears to the Vernons' argument, which lasted until they entered the house where Georgina immediately took refuge in her study, instructing Vanessa to bring tea and join her.

She was dictating madly when Vanessa arrived and forgot to switch off when she exploded angrily: "That brother of mine is mad. None of this script'll be legible. That'll delight you, won't it, my strait-laced innocent? Being a passionate lover isn't your scene at all . . . more a shrinking violet."

Vanessa said dispassionately: "Sometimes you haven't a clue, my dear employer. Take a drink and stop taking it out on me, just because Fabian's soft about my sister. I didn't invite her and, what's more, I never would without conferring first."

Georgina frowned into her cup: "I've ruined that tape.

"I'll change it."

"Type the first part, it's good. Don't dare alter a word, or leave anything out. You think I don't notice, but I do and you'll be obliged to type the original on the fair copy."

Vanessa shrugged, thinking she couldn't care less any more what drivel she typed, but she changed her mind when she played back the tape, throwing it aside in disgust. How could Georgina portray the main characters behaving in such a depraved manner? It seemed a deliberate insult to Dominic and dragged the heroine down to the gutter.

"I can't type this. It's filth. What will Dominic think when he reads it?"

Georgina had stretched cat-like onto a velvet-covered sofa, her long fair hair almost reaching the ground. Lazily she murmured: "But darling, Dom never reads anything I write. He was reared on the highbrow stuff from childhood. Uncle J. never allows fiction to desecrate his stuffy library collection." Sitting up, she added in teasing mockery: "How quick you are to jump to conclusions. Has it ever struck you as being conceited to read yourself into everything?"

Vanessa retorted stubbornly: "I'm not typing that tape. Why can't you realise such a novel as this will ruin your reputation?"

"That's all you know. Not only will it bring in a windfall, but no one will know I wrote it. A second pseudonym will be fun. Just get on with the typing, I'm dying to watch your face."

Vanessa typed, feeling sick, and, although she was tired, the lethargy which had helped over the past few weeks treacherously deserted, until her revulsion was too hard to control.

Snatching up the sheets of script she tore at them furiously, across and across until the fragments were tiny, spreading over the desk, the typewriter, her knees and the floor. Then she jumped up and made for the door, knowing she'd acted childishly, her cheeks flaming at the sound of Georgina's laughter.

She dreaded the thought that she would have to type the work again and wished, not for the first time, that Georgina would give way and install a word processor.

In the large kitchen, Vanessa slowly

relaxed, dealing expertly with vegetables from the farm, all beautifully fresh, the greens still slightly frosted. She had grown to appreciate the hour spent alone amongst spotless robots, silent and waiting patiently until the flick of a switch set them humming happily to her command. Thinking back to the chore of cooking in her stepfather's house, her mouth managed a smile. There she had lacked every amenity. Here, whatever Dominic thought of women, he had created a cook's delight she had yet to fault.

Her mind dwelling on the complex inmates of the house, it focused on Georgina who had at first intimidated and now raised compassion. It had taken several weeks for Vanessa to realise the older woman's permanent battle against frustration. The bouts of anger and extravagant poses were a necessary safety valve. She was in love with Dominic, had loved him from first meeting the raven-haired, chameleon boy who was completely unconscious of a woman's role. Vanessa's lips twisted again. Probably still was . . . except he now simply used them as a release for his virility. How many . . . ? She brought her thoughts to order. He was turned thirty and normal. She was the only one who had trapped him, a frightening admission knowing that when he was faced with an oncoming child he might hate its mother.

She had to be rational. She *had* to be. As Adrienne had pointed out there was no way of surviving without support.

It had grown very dark outside. A deft flick of the switch released the blinds, their descent smooth, giving time for a brief glimpse of golden eyes in a golden face watching with wistful intensity.

Reynard. Wiping her hands, Vanessa crossed to open the door, her feet almost swept from under her as the fox-cub leapt into the welcome warmth where he curled up in a corner.

"You," said Vanessa crossly, "will get me the sack. I've been warned about letting you into the house. Just pray no one finds out. Shuffle back a bit, I'll put a stool in front of you."

Stupid to talk to an animal but better than talking aloud to oneself. Vanessa continued preparations with a frown between her eyes. The animal had moved back obligingly. A coincidence, of course ... She glanced almost nervously into the corner and found two narrowed eyes staring at her with disturbing concentration.

She would not, she vowed, open the door to him again.

Janie arrived with a suitcase full of new clothes and a mood more ebullient than ever. "The tables have turned." She was over-excited, almost incoherent. "Steppa's got a woman and now he wants to get rid of me. Isn't it a scream? Who'd have thought the old stick-in-the-mud had it in him. She's all right too, took me to town shopping, spending *his* money. Oh, Vannie, I can't tell you how happy I am. I can't wait to marry

Fabian and live in this fabulous place. I will live here y'know."

Vanessa doubted it but decided to keep the peace. Not reminding her sister that this was Dominic's house, she merely murmured mildly that Fabian's domicile was on the borders of Wiltshire.

Janie shrugged that off: "Oh, but this place is so gorgeous. Now if he lived in the Cotswolds . . . but he'll move here if I ask him to, I know he will. He says he wants me to be happy. Oh, the same room, thanks." She dumped her case and ran to the window. "I can see the village rooftops and the horses. I shall learn to ride — Fabian does, but he says Dominic got rid of the horses. They had three, one each, but they were neglected when he went away. It was mean of him to sell, wasn't it? He could have hired someone to look after them . . . "

Vanessa privately thought that the Vernon brother and sister were at fault, leaning too much on their benefactor when neither of them were destitute.

She wondered if he ever tired of the responsibilities thrust on him. Tired in the physical sense, no doubt.

And was he tired now — tired of the danger and the dust, of living amongst hostilities with little to choose between ally and foe?

Where are you now, Dominic — sunning in Cyprus, trapped in a religious war ... or where nothing can touch you any more?

She waited but nothing materialised. How could she hope to reach him when they had nothing in common!

Janie came out of the bathroom. "Sheer luxury," she sighed: "lovely, soft, matching towels, expensive toiletries. You are used to it but can you imagine how much I want to live here?"

"No," Vanessa said dutifully.

"It's heaven to me, absolute heaven. But I ... well I must, simply must stay. Don't you agree?"

Vanessa looked at her sister, at the bright, expectant eyes and fair, pleading face, and felt a hundred years older instead of two. Knowing she should dash Janie's hopes, the habit of years made her hesitate. It was up to Fabian to install reason, and he must do so if he wanted a peaceful union.

With the advent of Janie, Georgina retired to her study. Vanessa had retyped the torn manuscript with several differences and not received comment, a significant fact. Georgina was mourning the loss of her man.

The days passed pleasantly, Janie in a placid mood, accepting without rancour the two vetoes placed on her: one, to keep clear of the hill; and two, to leave Reynard alone, after she complained he had snarled at her.

Fabian took it into his head to teach both Vanessa and Janie to drive and sat with each in turn as they drove up and down the long drive. They were so different, he said; one too fast and the other too careful. But they had many laughs over 'kangaroo' petrol and premature halts when gears were misused. Asked who was progressing the best he refused to reply, saying neither would pass a test, even with a blindfolded inspector. But he promised to persevere.

Vanessa took up knitting. She found the long dark nights an ordeal and unearthed a box of wool she had come across in one of the smaller attics. Using patterns from the stack of magazines accumulated by Georgina and, sitting up in bed, Vanessa created small, delightful garments, finding the occupation soporific and the faint smell of lavender pleasant.

Whose wool? she wondered. The first Mrs Russell's knitting contentedly before the arrival of the son who had robbed her of life? She must have lived here in this semi-paradise, in love with Jeff, the charming twin, looking forward to a long future. Prosaically, Vanessa concluded, the poor lady had died with her illusions unshattered.

Then, another tiny jacket finished, she hid it with the others before snuggling into bed, eyelids heavy with sleep.

The calm lasted for six days. Vanessa awoke heavy with premonition and from the moment she drew back the curtains and witnessed the strange phenomenon of a pale sun struggling through the creeping mist, she knew it was to be a bad day.

Adrienne telephoned immediately she got to the office: "Tony's back." She was subdued rather than jubilant. "He called from the airport and sounded terrible. I'm going to meet him — he hasn't any money. I asked about Dominic but he wouldn't say, seemed almost in tears. Vanessa, I'm sorry I can't put your mind at rest, but I promise to phone as soon as I get anything concrete. Maybe he was just too tired to talk. Let's look on the bright side like my foster mother always said."

The anguish of uncertainty settled over the house. Fabian went up to his attic; Georgina, already restless, paced the patio in the icy cold; and Janie hung over Vanessa's shoulder when she was trying to catch up with the latest batch of inspiration.

"I wish to goodness Adrienne would phone." Janie had not succumbed to the others' depth of anxiety, having little knowledge of the situation. Hurt because of Fabian's desertion, she sounded too much like a petulant child to do anything but inflame Vanessa's already raw nerves.

"Find something to do," she snapped. "I'm trying to concentrate."

"You can't be very worried if you can concentrate on that stuff."

"I said trying to, and stop reading over my shoulder."

Janie sprawled into the nearest chair. "You're all soon fed up with being nice. It won't make any difference though."

Exasperated, Vanessa asked: "Any difference to what? I wish you wouldn't talk in riddles."

"Any difference to me staying."

"Another riddle."

"No it's not, you know very well what

I mean. I'm staying here and no one is going to stop me. I came with the intention of staying. You can't turn me out and Fabian won't, so you've just got to fix Georgina between you. Actually she can't tell me to go — it isn't her house."

Aghast, Vanessa exclaimed: "And it isn't yours. Honestly, Janie, you're being ridiculous. You can't simply park yourself on other people. While Dominic is away, Georgina holds sway, that's taken for granted. If she says go, you go. Where's your pride anyway?"

"I haven't any. I've never been allowed any. I've been pushed around and I'm sick of it. Now I'm having my say. I'm staying here and that's that."

Vanessa gave up trying to finish her work and slammed the cover over the typewriter. No one had eaten any lunch but it was now nearing four o'clock and tea seemed in order. At least a drink would be welcome.

Trying to divert a head-on collision, she said: "Come and help to draw curtains and make tea. I'm in no fit state to reason with you. All I'm doing is listening for the phone. Please, Janie. Try to understand."

"That's what I want from you, understanding." Janie crossed to the window. "Just remember that I won't be put off. If I'm turned from here I'll kill myself." It was an unfortunate moment to choose dramatics and both Janie and Vanessa turned in startled guilt as Georgina spoke from the open door:

"You'll *what*! My God what a damn fool girl you are. Fabian must be out of his mind to consider marrying you. I'd class you as infantile. You've no sense and no reason. In fact, you are utterly selfish, Jane Meredith."

Vanessa could have told Janie that Georgina was dramatising a new character, but the girl leapt in without discretion before she was cautioned: "And you are . . . " she hissed . . .

Vanessa cowardly pressed her hands over her ears and it was into this amazing brawl that Fabian walked. As a bleak silence fell, he said one word to Vanessa: "Telephone," and she ran past him, white-faced, to snatch up the receiver, Georgina at her heels.

"It's all right." Adrienne's voice sounded strained. "Dominic's all right. He sent Tony back because he was no longer needed."

"Why hadn't Tony any money?" Vanessa's icy spine gave her no reassurance.

"The silly left his wallet in his coat."

"He flew back without his coat ... "

Adrienne exclaimed, sounding nervous: "Stop picking up red herrings, I've told you what you want to know. And I'll have to ring off, I'm on the works phone. If I hear anything more I'll phone from home. 'Bye."

Georgina, her ear to Vanessa's cheek, had picked up the message. "Not very lucid," she said. "Are you reassured? — because I'm not. That girl is holding something back."

Janie was missing and Fabian had

made the tea. As they sipped without tasting, he observed soberly: "I'd better fetch Janie, she was crying. Make up with her, George, or let her make up with you. She will grow up y'know."

Georgina watched her brother go, her lips curled: "She'll stay over my dead body. I can't stand the girl and, before you rise to her defence, if you're honest you'll agree there'd be no peace in this house with her around."

Vanessa said wearily: "It's all too much . . . " and received a sharp glance and the immediate retort that they were all in it, not just Vanessa who was, after all, an employee. Then Georgina made a grotesque grimace:

"Dear heaven, acid drips from my tongue these days. To hell with men, let's have a double and drown our sorrows. Fabian can sort out Jane, he invited her, and I promise not to say another word to her . . . " — she grimaced again — "except to say goodbye."

The tightness of Vanessa's lips eased.

She deplored the brawl but her sympathies were with her employer. It seemed Janie's confession, after four years, had severed the final link between them. Had her younger sister showed the slightest sign of contrition it might have been different. But Janie was, as accused by Georgina, utterly selfish.

The drink didn't reach the pouring stage, Fabian's hasty return setting alarm signals once more. Janie hadn't answered to his call and she wasn't to be found anywhere else in the house.

He said anxiously: "She can't have gone out in this mist. Vanessa, will you . . . ?"

Vanessa found her sister about to leave by the front door.

"Janie," she said sharply, "Janie . . . "

"I'm going and nothing you say will stop me. As if you'd want to anyway. You and that awful writer woman are in league, I know you are. I've left a letter for Fabian . . . " The high voice rose alarmingly, "As for, you, dear sister, I hope I never see you ever again."

Vanessa moved swiftly across the hall, reaching out, but was too late to grab Janie's arm. In desperation she ran outside and heard a disembodied voice floating back: "You won't catch me. I'm going to throw myself off the ledge."

Forgetting common sense and all warnings, Vanessa followed in the direction of the wild declaration. She didn't believe Janie would actually carry out her threat but she did realise there was a distinct possibility of unwary feet stumbling on the icy surface of the border path. A slip that could send Janie tumbling headlong down the rocky slope.

Despairingly she called her sister's name and heard, in answer, a scream of pure terror.

"Janie . . . "

Vanessa called again but there was no reply and, heart thumping sickeningly, she stopped on the track, willing her ears to pick up a sound.

But there was no sound, no sight, only a thick white blanket paralysing all senses, the damp, clinging horror penetrating hair, clothes and skin.

She was on the path, that's all she knew, all sense of direction lost. Putting out a hand she felt nothing but space. Perhaps, if she took a step sideways ... A shiver passed up her spine. The rail should be there. If she reached for it, and fell, would Dominic be sorry for not organising the long overdue repair? If she fell she wouldn't be killed but injured ... and that meant the baby too.

Vanessa swallowed her fright and shouted: "Janie! Wherever you are stand still, don't move a step. Try to guide me by calling my name. Call me and keep on calling. D'you hear, Janie? Say if you hear me."

In ghastly mimicry her words came back, trapped with her in a vacuum. She shivered again and heeded the warning. To stand still was suicide, her thin woollen jumper and skirt no protection against the freezing temperature.

But which way to go with no rail to

guide! Had Janie reached the plateau. Vanessa closed her mind against the other possibility.

How far up had she herself come. A third of the way. Half the way. There was shelter of sorts behind the big rock, a rough den that had survived the years. Dominic had made it. "To hide from George," Fabian had confided. "She always wanted to be with us and sometimes it was a bore."

Poor Georgina.

Vanessa slid a foot forward and encountered solid earth. One step up. Something to hang on to would be a godsend. Feel again for the rail. No rail within arm's length. A shoulder to lean on, she thought, and felt an insane desire to giggle. Nothing to lean on was what she had.

The cold was rapidly taking over, stiffening her legs and numbing her hands. She moved again and stopped, almost tumbling backwards. Space. She must move over to the left, not too far, there were boulders and trees. She stumbled into a boulder nevertheless and had to fight hard to control hysterical panic.

Think of *him*. Better not to. His eyes would darken with contempt at her stupidity. She was falling into one escapade after another, all her own lack of caution. She was just the kind he suffered unwillingly, the kind of brainless idiot who received a shot in the back by running into danger.

As she had done.

Oh, Dominic, I'm sorry. I wouldn't make a good wife for a man like you.

With a great effort of will, Vanessa pulled her scattered thoughts together, reviewing the situation with a kind of detached deliberation. Better to stand still, perhaps. Georgina and Fabian must be alerted by now. To go on would court certain disaster; not helping Janie, more likely causing injury to the baby. Vanessa badly wanted the baby. A precious reminder of a gentle lover who had nothing in common with Dominic Russell.

Vanessa tried and failed to be lucid. Then a grim trick of the ever-swirling mist brought a hopeless cry across the distance.

"Vannie, Vannie, we shall die like that other girl. Vannie . . . Vannie . . . Vannie . . . help me . . ."

The blanket closed down. Vanessa felt the urge to sit down, giving up. He would despise that too. Why couldn't she stop thinking of him? Where was he? Perhaps he would never know the mother of his child was slightly insane.

Stupid thinking again. Did being trapped always do this to a human! Shaking her head in a bid to clear it, Vanessa took a cautious step forward and slipped on the sparse, mossy grass, only a frantic grab preventing a fall. The tree she was gripping bent under her weight and she felt her frozen fingers slide down the flaking bark until her knees met the ground. Was it an illusion or was the atmosphere warmer . . . and worse, a cotton wool substance filling her eyes, nose and mouth, making her gasp for breath?

She cried out in terror for the man who had unwittingly taken over her life: "Dominic. Dominic. I'm afraid Dom-in-ic . . . " Something warm brushed her face, warm and wet . . . hairy.

Reynard.

The journey back to the house was sheer hell. Reynard kept running ahead, impatient at her slowness. But he always returned when she stopped and, on one occasion, actually nuzzled her hand.

Vanessa found herself talking aloud to him and was half way through a sentence when a large car-rug was thrown about her shoulders and her arm was seized in a fierce grip.

"Dear heaven, you're delirious," said Georgina's voice.

"Not. Talking to Reynard."

"In that case you damn well are delirious. Let's get you inside. A bath, bed and whisky for you, my girl."

It sounded wonderful. No brickbats either. Georgina was usually fairly vitriolic with fools.

Vanessa asked faintly: "Have you . . . is Janie . . . ?"

"Fabian brought her in." That was all, still no searing condemnation.

And later, when the ordeal of humanising was over, Vanessa leaned thankfully on her pillows and said from the heart: "Thank you, Georgina."

"Um. If you knew what it cost me not to fly off the handle. Only thing is, I've found I hate you less than I thought."

"And that," Vanessa said, "is a step in the right direction. Would your current heroine have acted so stupidly?"

Georgina flounced to the window. "Not likely, she values her own skin too much. I've decided there's more in you than meets the eye."

That Vanessa thought, welcoming a shaft of humour, is more true than you know. Literally speaking.

10

DOMINIC had scarcely dumped his suitcase on the doorstep before Jonathan appeared, his bearded face as cheerful as always and his manner as jovial.

"You're late, you old bastard," was his greeting. "Leave that stuff. We're going fishing. A great haul offshore. And before you ask, I've no info for you yet. Too much milling about over there. A week or two in the sun for you and you look as if you darn well need it."

Friends since university days, formality was a foreign word. Dominic felt his inner turmoil lessen and turned to meet Gerda as she rushed out of the villa by one of the long windows.

"Dominic, darling, as handsome as ever. Give me a kiss ... right here, none of your cold English pecks. Hm, that's better; have you been practising? Is there a woman at last?"

Dominic winced inwardly. Telephoning his father from the airport he had learned that Vanessa had lied about not being pregnant and he didn't find the reason for this flattering, angry with his sense of loss as well as with finding another fault in a girl he thought about as little as he possibly could.

He picked up his luggage and Jon exclaimed impatiently: "Mayita'll take that to your room. Let's get going before it's too late."

Dominic retained his hold: "I've got to change. Ten minutes'll see me."

Ten minutes was more than enough. The sheer pleasure of uncharacteristically tossing aside formal wear was a further step to relaxation. Thin slacks and shirt, no socks inside leisure shoes. Shorts would come after acclimatising. He could do without too many sarcastic comments about his pale skin. Whatever they wore on one of these pleasure trips, they always ended up soaked, one or the other tipping up the glass-bottomed boat, throwing everything, including their catch, into the blue water. "Poor beggars," Jon would comment, watching the fish make a frantic escape. "They should be thankful we don't use barbaric hooks for them to live with the rest of their lives." Soft inside was Jonathan Perry.

Everything happened as usual except that, as they lay sunning on the bank, Jonathan asked lazily: "What would your father say to us letting the fish go?"

"Haven't a clue. Why ask such a damn silly question?"

"Dunno. He phoned before you came but I wasn't home. Gerda took the call but she got nothing out of him."

"Why didn't you say, I'd have made contact."

"Didn't want you to then. You can when we get back."

Dominic turned on his side and regarded the guileless expression on Jon's face accusingly. But he let the matter drop, knowing full well what his reasoning would be. It had happened before, this heart-warming protectiveness. Another nudge towards relaxation. He settled back again, shielding his eyes from the sun: "Did I look as foul as all that?"

"Worse than foul. Sent down."

Dominic laughed and was surprised at the sound. There really wasn't much for him to laugh about. "You old fool," he contented himself by saying, but his problems suddenly seemed manageable again. Jon had that effect on him.

Ten minutes later they were swimming strongly out to sea, the clear, cool water a refreshing tonic, a world apart from war. For once they didn't fool about, Jon seeming reluctant and Dominic enjoying the pull of muscles long denied invigorating exercise.

Once away from this idyllic spot and in the Lebanon he knew the going would be tough. He needed to be fit. Turning on his back he closed his eyes and summarised the position. To gain access should present no problem. To dismantle the machine could be a lengthy job. To get away, if Pelham did his sums right, shouldn't be too tricky. Dominic sighed. Pelham was the weak link. He was already showing signs of panic. One slip in the timing and they might end up amongst the hostages.

Dominic turned over and beachwards, following Jon who was already halfway back. Hostage, he thought, and quickened his pace. He had heard a great deal about their treatment and decided he'd rather be dead.

The evening was growing chilly as they walked to the villa and Dominic was glad to take a shower, relieving his aching joints as well as warming up. Then he telephoned his father to no avail: a message was delivered by Henry, the manservant, simply a reminder to keep in close contact, if possible once a day.

Some chance of that, Dominic thought as he went into the Perrys' pleasant living-room. For a day or two perhaps.

After the evening meal, they played snooker, Jonathan, as always, the winner, and Gerda an onlooker supplying generous drinks. It wasn't until she left to put their youngest child to bed that Jon called a halt, marched pointedly into his office and directed Dominic to the one easy chair. Jon sat behind his desk, slumped comfortably and, fixing an eagle eye, demanded: "Out with it. Tell all."

About to deny there was 'all' to tell, Dominic changed his mind and said briefly: "Woman trouble."

"When have you not had?"

"This is serious. I'll have to marry her."

Jon's golden eyes widened: "You randy devil." Then in surprise: "You, of all people. Are you joking?" As Dominic shook his head, Jonathan demanded: "What the blazes were you doing, apart from the obvious. You must have been mad." Curiosity took over: "What's she like?"

What was she like? Dominic thought

of Vanessa's glorious hair, of the irritating unawareness in her eyes, of the lips that didn't know how to respond. He couldn't describe her, not as a whole. He said lamely: "All right, if you mean how does she look."

"Don't tell me she's dumb? Sounds as if she must be . . . or was it a bait? . . . Women do catch idiots like you, no caution. I suppose you were drunk."

Dominic left the chair and wandered to the window, appreciating the lowering sun and the brightness of the stars, even while he tried to assemble lucidity. From behind, Jonathan asked: "As you're so enthusiastic can't you get out of it, buy her off, suggest an abortion . . . "

Something snapped inside Dominic. He swung round, angry now, wanting to defend the girl who had given with such generosity. "No!" he said fiercely, "never that. Never either of those. She isn't one of those women. I couldn't let her down. And I don't know if she will marry me. Maybe she hates my guts."

Jonathan held up a placating hand: "Okay, okay, little brother, pipe down. Sounds a case of another chap falling into the tender trap. Hook, line and sinker at that. The calm, collected young Russell. I'll allow she must be something if she got inside your rigid code of behaviour. What has the father figure to say about the *contretemps*? I assume you've told him?"

"Why not?" Dominic moderated his tone and walked back to sit on the edge of the desk, one leg swinging restlessly. "He knows Vanessa, she's Georgina's secretary."

"And does he approve?"

"I don't know whether he does or not." Anger rose again: "I wish everyone didn't assume he rules my life. He never has and he never will."

"He sends you on all these lousy jobs."

"That's my choice. I enjoy them." Until now, thought Dominic bleakly. This was different, a fool's errand

. . . the child. He smashed down on his thoughts, flooded with relief as Gerda crept with exaggerated caution into the room. He liked his friend's wife, admiring her subtle handling of difficult situations and intrigued by her effortless management of a pilot husband and four healthy offsprings. His anger fizzled out as she blew him a kiss.

"Don't let the big bear bully you, sweetheart," she said. "And regarding marriage he's infantile. I run this shop and he just pays." Her generous mouth curled mischievously at their combined surprise. "Lucy's bedroom has a balcony above the window and she insists on saying her prayers outside. If you boys only knew what secrets I hear while I'm supposed to be listening to higher things." She moved lightly and patted Dominic's knee: "Marriage isn't so bad, and if there's not enough love, money paves the way. You, dear Dominic, have plenty. You'll have a fortunate child and, who knows, you might even like it."

Jon came in with the last comment before he swept them out of his office: "I'm wondering if Vanessa will?"

It was early morning before sleep laid down a welcome blanket and, even then, Dominic slept lightly, disturbed by disconnected dreams. By eight o'clock he was speaking to a sleepy Tony Pelham and was not reassured by the string of complaints. Ignoring the expected ones, he seized curtly on the financial angle, appalled at the reckless spending.

"We have a limited bank account. Go easy. Take your meals in the hotel."

"I was fed up of staying in. It's all right for you." Into the stony silence, Tony said unhappily: "Sorry, sir, I didn't mean ... Well, what I mean is, I don't know anyone in this place and there's a hell of a racket going on even at this hour."

"What kind of a racket?"

"Shouting and gunfire."

"You're out of the zone. Keep a low profile. I'll be back as soon as I get the go-ahead. Nothing has come through yet." Dominic stood for a moment frowning at the dead receiver. One thing was certain. He must get back to Beirut before Pelham blew a fuse.

A high, little voice from the region of his knees asked: "What're you scowling at, Modic? You'll spoil your face." Gaining his attention she gave the unnecessary information: "I've only got my knickers on. I have to when men are around."

Dominic eyed the small infant warily. Not having enjoyed his experience of children he was at a loss how to answer the candid statement. He said the first thing that occurred: "Don't you wear knickers anyway?" and swung round in embarrassment as, from the kitchen archway, Gerda gave a squeal of amusement, bringing the colour to his face.

"What an enlightening conversation so early in the day. Darling Dominic, you're blushing and I didn't think that possible. Come and have some coffee."

To her precocious four-year-old she said: "Let go of Uncle Dom's sleeve and go to Mayita. She's waiting for you."

Lucinda rebelled: "Want to be with Modic. He's a man."

Her mother said drily: "Glad you know the difference, my sweet baby. Off you go, you can torment the man for the remainder of the day, by the swimming-pool. Daddy and I are going shopping." Eyes full of mischief she regarded Dominic. "A little forerunner of things to come."

But over breakfast she talked to him seriously, without bias, pointing out a woman's side of a commitment and accepting frankly that a liaison was mutual, if not a little tilted in the lady's direction.

"Vanessa must like you a lot to have let you into her bed," Gerda said. "And now tell me to mind my own business." Smiling at his blank expression she added: "But you're too much of a gentleman to do so. Y'know, dear Dominic, you are quite an unusual breed. Not quite human."

"And that," he retorted, "is the compliment of the year. Are you scheming to humanise me?"

"No, I'll leave that to another woman whose name you know very well and neither Jon nor I will mention again unless you invite us to. One thing though, we appreciate your confidence. Jon says he's always been a safety valve."

Dominic refilled both their cups. He was usually inured to Gerda's outspokenness but this time she'd struck home. Vanessa's side of the affair was being hammered into him. She had called his attitude selfish once before and he hadn't liked the adjective.

Was that how she was feeling now? How did a twenty-two-year-old girl face up to the future? Alone.

The telephone summoned and it was Jonathan from the airport base. Succinctly he said: "All clear. Go ahead and, little brother, take care, you'll be in a tricky situation. The media have moved on for some reason or other, stopped clearing the factory site. From inside reports the access to the cellar is still available to anyone aware of it. Get a move on. See you when the mission is over. And don't muff it. There's a flight in an hour. Get Gerda to run you in. I'm off on an inland flight so can't help."

Dominic caught the plane and met Pelham at the arranged venue.

11

MAKING little effort to keep the tremor from his voice, Tony Pelham said: "We're trapped, aren't we? That fellow might come down here at any moment. Why hasn't he?"

"He's waiting for reinforcements," Dominic spoke curtly. He was weary of being a prop to a man on the verge of panic. Another of them. Was it impossible to find a reliable aide, one who accepted the best way to deal with a hazardous situation was to keep calm?

Feeling in his pocket he felt the smooth shell of the detonator alongside the slim, powerful torch. So far the emergency generator had held out, one blessing; everything else seemed to be going wrong. Why had Jon given the all-clear when a fresh troop was moving in? He wondered if he'd ever know.

The machine was set back snugly into a recess which, in fact, made his task more difficult, having limited elbow room. To dismantle the facia needed a delicate touch in full light. The heavily sealed, secret units were behind the electronics and these he had to get at in order to place the explosive device.

Afterwards they had fifteen minutes to get out. Fifteen! Long enough if the way was clear and Pelham didn't fumble about as he was apt to do when under stress. The man was always losing equipment. One day he'd lose his head in more ways than one. An unfortunate observation and Dominic smiled grimly. What a hell of a jam they were in. Sheer bad luck the reinforcements had moved in so swiftly; something no one could have foreseen, although it wasn't like Jon to make a slip.

Pelham was chipping at the mud wall with a fingernail, making Dominic tense to exasperation. The fellow was going to be useless in a tight corner;

he would be better without him. There was still a good chance of him getting past the man at the exit who was pacing up and down indecisively. Decisive himself, Dominic said: "Get out while you have the chance."

Tony Pelham backed against the mud wall: "Don't send me up into that hell."

"It'll be a bigger hell down here if we get trapped, you fool."

Tony shuddered, visibly: "I hate this game. I didn't want to come."

"And I didn't want you, you're gutless."

"We can't all be like you, rock-hard, no feelings . . . "

Dominic said in suppressed fury: "Get going while the tunnel is still open. Once out, don't belt across open ground as Paxton did and get a bullet in the back. Keep to the perimeter and mingle with the crowd. Take off your jacket and leave it down here and pull your shirt out of your trousers. Look as scruffy as you can."

"But my wallet. I've nowhere to keep it except in my jacket."

Dominic strove grimly for patience. "D'you value money more than life? You have your papers safe, I hope."

"Sewn into my pants, but — "

In a burst of rage, Dominic exclaimed: "Throw your jacket down and get out."

Every second was precious. He watched Pelham stumbling away and then swore profusely as the lights went out. That was all he needed. Feeling in his pocket he drew out the miniature torch, a poor substitute when handling tricky electronics, not much help at all, but he knew the monster off by heart. And hated it. To render it useless was a pleasure. The one back home was much more sophisticated, such improvement making it unnecessary to train other men to use this old model which he, alone, could handle.

He had just commenced the arduous task of removing the facia when cold steel thrust at his throat and the growling command to keep still was not needed. He stood still, not praying. Icy cold. Numb! His thoughts scattered wildly and hardly made sense. He wished he didn't know so much about the treatment of hostages. His mind sheered away and he thought of the baby. Of Vanessa he didn't think at all. A woman's machinations scared him.

Scared. The metal at his head prodded him backwards until his back was to the wall.

"Armed?"

"No."

"Hard cheese."

Dominic agreed but a faint ray of hope came. The man was an American, not an Arab. He had to be a mercenary. Tentatively he said: "I've money . . . " The nuzzle jerked painfully and his natural reaction was to throw up an arm. A second later, a shot pierced his ears. Blood cascaded over him, punctuating the blackness with red streaks and soaking his shirt, oozing, sticky, hot. He waited for pain, for his legs to give way and, instead, almost collapsed under the weight of his captor as the inert body slumped downwards.

The fool had shot himself. That upward jerk ... he'd had the trigger cocked. The danger was that the shot might have been heard, or the roof cave in from the vibration. Fighting nausea he moved carefully, avoiding the body at his feet. All that blood. The man had got to be dead. In any case ... Dominic disciplined his thoughts to the job in hand. He had demonstrated and recovered machines from all over the world, the most tricky in Saudi Arabia; but this one with, virtually, a gun at his head, held the most danger. As he dismantled with delicate precision, he mused over the reason he had stayed loyal to the man who considered it a weakness to show the slightest sign of approval. He grimaced, knowing the same old answer would emerge. For one thing he had no other relation, discounting his real father. The Russell twins had been inseparable until the advent of a woman. Four years old at the time, he had hidden all over the house to avoid the acrimonious reaction of his uncle. Disloyalty rang from every rafter. John Russell had lost a much loved wife and an equally loved brother.

Dominic didn't know how long it was before he'd been captured in the stables, hauled up into Sam's horsey embrace and carried into the study where his uncle sat like a frozen image at the knee-hole desk which was ideal for shaping a den. Dominic couldn't remember whether he had snivelled or been afraid. What he recalled was his own explosion of protest to the man he had never much liked. "Sam says I'm going to get a damned good hiding. I won't be hitted."

And the grim reply: "I shall never lay hands on you, Dominic, not in my lifetime. But I'm going to be your father from now on and I'll expect obedience and loyalty. And the word is 'hit'."

The last slim wire came away and Dominic felt in his pocket for the other small object he carried: incredibly tiny and powerfully lethal, with enough mechanical force to blow up the whole fortification, let alone the machine, him also if he didn't get out. Once detonated, the safety time limit was fifteen minutes.

Dominic shone the torch beam around the cellar, memorising the quickest way to the tunnel. The soldier lay where he had fallen, not bloody. He had expended his life over Dominic and the restricting stiffness was revolting. 'Do the job properly,' had been the old man's order. 'There is value in the construction even after the electronic system is destroyed.' Dominic knew more of the computer's workings than John Russell did but he rarely retaliated. A habit of over twenty years dies hard . . . if ever.

He was at the foot of the slope when a flashing light and a shout from above halted him. Cursing his own stupidity he moved cautiously backwards intent on finding the soldier's gun. Although familiar with firearms he had avoided carrying one, was squeamish of taking life. Not a James Bond at all, he thought grimly as he turned the body over, not cut out for this game: I'd rather be a farmer and settle in the country. Settle with whom? Vanessa and the coming baby? He would have to marry her, of course.

The gun was evasive, must have slid across the ground. Too late he shone his torch and was blinded by a beam from a much more powerful lamp.

"Stand still."

The demand was becoming monotonous. He stood still, suffering the same routine, menacing metal thrust roughly into his throat. Inwardly he prayed for another mercenary but doubted such luck.

"Where the hell is Corny? Who the hell are you?" The beam swept the cellar, pausing on the body, and a spurt of obscenity poured from the man's lips: "You bastard, you've killed him. He was my buddy. We've worked together for fifteen years. I'll kill you.

I'll make you squeal, you . . . " With another burst of obscenity, the soldier swung the rifle in an arc, contacting with an ominous crack. "Now try to shoot me, you — "

Dominic said painfully: "I'm not armed."

"Then how in Hades . . . ? You're English."

"Yes."

The rifle was fractionally withdrawn: "What goes?"

"Dismantling a machine."

"And have you?"

"Not quite. There are sealed units. I've detonated."

"How long?" The torch beam swung to illuminate the defaced machine.

"Fifteen minutes. Ten now."

"And the tunnel is caving in, that's why I came after Corny. Just get going. The DPs'll love carving you up."

"Leave me . . . "

"Not likely. One Brit hostage'll net a thousand dollars."

Through his teeth, Dominic said:

"You've smashed my arm. If I move I shall pass out."

"You'll pass out anyway. Stop whining. Get going."

Activated by rifle and boot, Dominic managed to keep his feet. They were within yards of the exit when the world disintegrated, catapulting the mercenary on to his back. Face downwards in the choking dust and badly handicapped, trapped by the weight of a body and reinforced clay debris, Dominic decided to give up. There was no longer a guiding light and every breath was agonising. It was a hellish way to die but better than falling into the terrorists' hands.

Lethargy clamped. He was soaked by sweat, couldn't feel any more. No pain, only darkness.

Incongruously the soldier choked into Dominic's ear. "Keep going, Bud. For God's sake go on. I'm trapped . . . can't get past you."

"Go to hell." There was no incentive. Prods no longer registered.

The man gasped hoarsely: "Haven't you got a dame?"

"No."

"Someone?"

"No."

"A kid?"

"No, damn you." He didn't want anyone. He didn't want a child to be born into this hell hole of a world. He didn't want to be married, to see the look of strain and anxiety in eyes that should be smiling. She'd had her troubles . . .

The soldier gasped: "I'll see you over the line . . . hospital base." His voice grew less intelligible: "Go . . . on . . . you . . . do it . . . few yards . . . go . . ."

Lungs bursting, Dominic put his head on his good arm and listened in vague wonder to the clamouring of voices. Foreign. So they had got him after all and he didn't give a damn. The illusion faded, he absorbed the mercenary's pleas without reaction. Was the soldier of fortune on his knees? Poor devil.

The guttural moans became muted, softened, effeminate, whispering his name: 'Dominic.'

He was hallucinating. Vanessa was safe in the shelter of his beautiful hills where the heather glowed in the sun and the mist hovered like a benevolent blanket.

Vanessa! It was as if she touched him, that shy, tentative touch, ready to recoil at the slightest move on his part. Right about the hair, though ... unleashed passion, given generously when gentled into arousal. She'd cope alone — better, without a man, such as himself. And he'd made adequate provision.

As his father had. Both fathers ... giving everything except an ear to youthful uncertainties.

'Dominic,' she said in anguish, 'Dom-in-ic ... Help me. I'm afraid.'

She was afraid! He was lily-livered. A sobering thought when he had struggled all his life not to admit weakness.

The voices faded. Breathing was sheer agony. He must have air a any price. His good hand clawed forward and the weight slid off his back. Without conscious compassion, Dominic reached back to drag his companion on. There was still no light but the debris was thinner. Another pull. Then another . . . The nightmare worsened. They lay under open sun, the soldier barely conscious; both of them were fighting for breath; just another two men joining the row of casualties dragged from the debris. Except for Dominic they were all mercenaries and, with them, he was eventually carried off to the hospital base, the agony of being moved beyond endurance.

For a while events became blurred and he existed in confused isolation. In this cosmopolitan community few were interested in a supposed mercenary with a mere broken arm and congested lungs, both of which would mend. Other injuries took precedence; terrible wounds gaping from contact with flying masonry. They, although few were fatal, drew immediate attention. Dominic's injuries were invisible and he was left to suffer with 'recover and get to hell out of here,' the advice. Beds were short, linen and toiletries a barely existent luxury.

The mercenary, with only a sack of straw, told Dominic that supplies weren't getting through and urgent drugs were desperately scarce. 'Best thing is to get out.' He wrote the message on a pad. 'Got anywhere to go?' He scribbled again. 'Keep away from the centre. Fad's thugs are out in force. Stick to the perimeter and keep your head down.'

Next morning he had gone and Dominic left his bed without wanting to collapse, a considerable improvement. Balance still at variance, he had nothing to carry and was still clad in bloodied, filthy rags — a blessing in disguise, for the streets were full of rebels with trigger-happy fingers ready to pick out the affluent.

Many hours later, it seemed to him, he reached the hotel and was refused admission, humiliatingly ejected from the foyer before he was given breathing-space. Unable to speak, he could only lean on the iron rail at the side of the steps and struggle with the threatening faintness. His broken arm was numb but the lacerations of his clawing hand was tearing him apart. He thought in helpless despair that he was in danger of losing both arms if he didn't receive medical treatment before the day was out.

The doorman came down to him, aggressively hostile. "Move off before I call the police," he said.

Desperation giving strength, Dominic fumbled for his papers and received a stunning blow to the side of his head. He slid into unconsciousness trying to say for the third time that he wasn't armed.

Ten days later, Dominic caught the afternoon flight to Cyprus, arriving at the villa to find Jon away on a long flight and Gerda in England visiting her three sons. Lucinda and Mayita were the only occupants, the latter thrown into confusion at the sight of a gaunt Englishman with a bandaged hand, an arm in a sling and barely enough breath to speak.

Feeling an interloper, Dominic asked if he might stay for a few days and was answered by the precocious baby, who gave her approval in a manner endearingly like her mother.

"Your clothes are here, Modic. You can have the same room. You're just in time for tea. We can sit by the pool."

The suggestion was a balm. Dominic felt the surprising urge to give the child a kiss. After the rigours of hospital, a marking time in this peaceful haven seemed like heaven.

Lucilla was saying haughtily: "I'm Priscilla."

"Lucilla," he corrected.

"No. Priscilla."

He argued no more. It really didn't concern him what the child liked to call herself. Instead he fell asleep on a comfortable lounger and wakened to burning discomfort. Cursing his own fool hardiness, he sat up to stare towards the distant hill; so different from those at home, pastel instead of purple and blue-spattered green. A tug of longing made him sigh. A few days to convalesce and he would be off. But off to what? A worried father, upset by not receiving the expected contact. A baby in the offing. The terrifying prospect of marriage.

To Dominic, in his low state, the future was bleak. He found it impossible to believe that Gerda and Jon's relationship was permanent.

He groaned aloud and started as a small voice said from beside him:

"I fetched the sunburn oil. You shouldn't go to sleep in the sun."

"I shouldn't," he agreed meekly. "It was a mistake."

"Are you very tired?"

"Not now. What happened to the tea?"

"Mayita took it away. I've made you a cold drink."

"Thanks."

She was sitting cross-legged, showing a wealth of chubby body tanned to a downy peach. Candid eyes, cheeky nose ... He picked up the oil and dabbed savagely.

'Oh, Vanessa,' he thought, 'I'll make a lousy husband.'

12

VANESSA turned from surveying the dripping landscape and saw him there. The same! Immaculate, straight-backed, expression, in the dimness of the room, as guarded as she could remember.

Words refused to come. Heart a great pain, she stared, drinking in his presence, hardly believing he was real. Then, eyes becoming accustomed to the gloom, she noticed the empty jacket sleeve, the darkness of his hollowed eyes and his gaunt body.

Dominic asked wryly: "No greeting, Vanessa?"

Her lips parted, but words lodged in the dryness of her throat and she could only make a small gesture of helplessness.

The shadow in the doorway moved forward. Mr John Russell put a hand under his son's elbow. Tone harsh, he said: "Now come along. You've had your way and now it's time for mine." Cold eyes assessed and dismissed Vanessa's rigid stance. He exclaimed impatiently: "We're wasting time, Dominic."

For a brief moment, Dominic resisted, his appraisal of her white face less critical. The amusement there, but very faint, he said: "I've been hearing about your escapades, young Meredith. Too many of them but we'll forget those. Why did you lie about the baby?"

Lie about the baby! How did he know there was to be one? Stricken, she watched them leave, seeing Dominic stumble, and choked on tears that refused to come. She had held them back so long. Now they were denied her.

Life came into her feet and she ran across the hall, wrenching open the great oak door. They were already in the car, the driver in his seat and, even as she gave an anguished call, he drove off, leaving her on the step, desperately afraid for Dominic and more alone than ever.

An irate Georgina dragged her in, slamming the door with a violence indicative of her feelings.

"He's gone, it's no use standing there letting the cold in. Why the drama? What's wrong with you?"

Vanessa crept to a chair and crumpled into it, shaking visibly. "I let him go, Georgina. I didn't say a word. It was such a shock, seeing him unexpectedly and then finding he was ill. He was angry about . . . oh, everything. How did he know?"

Georgina sat on the chair-arm: "More like exhausted, poor lamb. He should have gone straight into hospital but he's a stubborn idiot. Came to see you, I suppose."

"How did he know about all the things I'd done?"

"I wrote and told him it was time he took some of the responsibility off me."

Vanessa thrust back her hair in

frustration. "I don't know what anyone is talking about. I — " Breaking off she said slowly: "So you know about the baby too. How?"

"Uncle J. told me, so, presumably, he told Dominic. Quite concerned was the old man, you dashing into every kind of madness. Told me to watch over you or words to that effect. And if you want to know where he had the information from, the answer is simple. Men have a way of noticing a woman is pregnant; he suspected and telephoned our dear Doctor Malcolm, who was only too delighted to pass on the good news."

In the ensuing silence, Vanessa said: "I wanted Dominic to be the first to know. It's a private thing between us. He's horrified, I know. He doesn't want to be tied down. I don't want to be a hanger-on."

"You," Georgina said forcibly, "are talking nonsense. He's as much to blame as you. More so, being an experienced man and you being a nitwit."

Vanessa asked in a whisper: "What's

wrong with Dominic?"

"From the little I got out of Uncle J., the damage is bad but mendable: arm badly set, crushed ribs and pneumonia."

Through clenched teeth, Vanessa said viciously: "Damned machines."

"Don't condemn them, my girl. They bring in the money."

"Money can't heal hurt."

"No. Oh, do be reasonable. You must accept that it's a necessary evil. Dominic'll get tip-top attention, pretty nurses to hold his hand and a fantastic convalescence of his choice. You with him, perhaps. But not if you don't shake yourself up and stop acting like a tragedienne. He's had his fun and he'll marry you because he's that kind of man."

Vanessa took a breath: "And you don't mind?"

"I mind about losing him but as it's you I can bear it." Georgina laughed and, in a surprising gesture of affection, ruffled Vanessa's hair. "Now go and cook a celebration meal. He's back in practically one piece and he's tough enough to mend quickly. Open champagne and we'll toast his recovery."

Vanessa spoke her thoughts aloud: "I want to go to him."

"Give the poor man a few days' respite. Knowing Dom well I happen to remember getting forcibly pushed out of his bedroom when he had chickenpox. He's as vain as hell."

Vanessa waited four soul-searching days. Then she rang the Russell residence, getting, as expected, Henry on the receiver. Firmly she asked him to fetch Mr Russell and was rewarded by immediate attention. "I'd like to see Dominic but I don't know where he is." Imagining him standing in the large, impersonal room she listened to the level voice giving the reluctant information, then asked with decreased confidence: "Can I visit?"

"Dominic likes to lick his wounds in private."

"Meaning that I won't be welcome?

Had I better ask?"

"If you ask he'll say no." A few seconds of bleak silence and then John Russell said: "Come if you wish, Vanessa. Here to me. I'll take you this afternoon."

Suffering second thoughts at the wisdom of her impulsive action, Vanessa rushed upstairs to eye the contents of her wardrobe with dissatisfaction. Lax over buying clothes she now regretted having to wear the much used green dress. But she had bought a new jacket and her shoes were good, although her handbag, bulging at the seams, was ancient and looked it. The remedy was simple. She would get an earlier train, have her hair cut and shaped, buy a new bag and dump the old one in a convenient litter bin. The idea of lunching with Adrienne she dismissed. Her friend was too involved with the recent painful episode. For the present they were on opposite sides, loyalties divided between two men, one who had deserted his post.

Using a different venue, Vanessa lunched alone and at two o'clock presented herself, handbag renewed and hair neatly coiffured, at the forbidding door of the Russell residence. Henry showed her to the daunting sitting-room, gave her coffee and regally departed saying Mr Russell would be with her shortly.

As she sipped, Vanessa tried to imagine a young boy living in such an atmosphere. Georgina had said that women were not employed so it was to be assumed that the cook was male. Irrelevantly she wondered if Henry ever let his hair down. Someone must have played with Dominic. Restlessly she wandered to the chiffonier and stood looking at the beautiful chess set. At the side was a thick pad, marked at the top with the letters S and D. Flicking underneath she came to the initials D and Dom and she felt an inward painful squeeze. Daddy and Dominic. But S, who was S? Whoever it was had not let Dominic win. Daddy had.

She was still standing in contemplation when John Russell came to her shoulder. He commented coolly:

"The chess set is Dominic's property. It was handed down through the family. He was too young to appreciate its worth for many years."

"Worth!" It was an angry reaction rather than a question.

"Not moneywise. Discipline and concentration."

Vanessa asked abruptly: "Who was S?"

"I was."

"Meaning sir?"

"Just that." As she looked up at him, he said quietly: "The boy found it difficult to replace my brother. He chose to use another form of address."

"He doesn't now?" Another tentative question.

"Only when he's annoyed with me."

The short conversation opened up a whole new understanding and Vanessa sat in thoughtful introspection during the journey to the hospital. Once there, and inside the clinical confines, her nervous system developed panic, making her entry into Dominic's room that of a mouse approaching annihilation.

Dominic appeared to be asleep. She closed the door softly and stood, back to the panels, willing her heartbeats to slow and her recent self-assurance to emerge. After all she had known intimacy with this man and was carrying his child. And he was helpless.

Moving quietly, Vanessa stopped at the bedside and felt again the painful constriction inside. He *was* helpless, confined by a saline drip and a heavily plastered arm. He looked ill, grey under the misleading sun-tan, dark lashes heavy on the hollowed cheeks. Tears burned behind her eyes and she wanted to run, remembering Georgina's warning. He would hate her to see him like this.

The nurse came in. She was young and pretty but entirely businesslike. "He shouldn't be having visitors yet," she said, setting down an ominously laden tray, "only family like his father. I dread anything that'll make him a worse patient than he already is. Keeping him down is a nightmare. He actually takes off the drip and, every morning, insists on using the bathroom when I could easily shave him."

Vanessa kept discreetly silent having seen Dominic's lips twitch. She could well believe him a bad patient and, in a way, it gave her relief. Somewhere she had heard said that the sick who were awkward weren't chronically ill; bloody-mindedness was far too strenuous an effort. Watching the nurse prepare a syringe, Vanessa asked meekly: "Is he sedated?"

"He has to be, and watched. I wouldn't put it past him to discharge himself." The nurse plunged in the syringe, making Dominic flinch.

"You needn't be so damned vicious," he said. "Go and rustle up some of your foul tea for this lady. She's carrying my baby."

She went, scarlet-faced and Vanessa

sat weakly on the convenient chair: "You," she exclaimed, "are outrageous. I prefer, Mr Russell, sir, not to be branded a prostitute."

He was regarding her with an unreadable expression, but his eyes were blue. "A curtain lecture already," he observed in mild mockery. "Will you marry me, Vanessa?"

Such unexpectedness took her breath away, aggravating rather than reassuring. Without stopping to think she shot back: "You must be under sedation if you think . . . " The amazing darkening of his eyes stifled the rest of the sentence and she said in shamed regret: "You ought not to be worrying about such serious things at the moment." Startled at his sudden impatience, she asked: "What are you doing? Dominic, don't!" But he ignored her protest and fumbled with the confining tube.

"Take this damn thing off me, I want to sit up. D'you hear, Vanessa."

She said flatly: "I hear but don't heed. Stop being obstructive. What's the damn thing for anyway?"

"Dehydration."

"Well then."

"I've enough water inside me to sink a battleship."

"This is a hospital and you are a patient."

"So what?" But he was less aggressive.

"So you aren't the big boss and have to do as they say."

"D'you know," he said, still mildly disagreeable, "you're talking like a wife." Then, not giving time for her reply: "Are we quarrelling or is it just me? Vanessa, please take this needle out of my arm, it's twisted and hurts like the devil. Thanks. You're more compassionate than my jailer."

"She's cross with you." Her gaze was suddenly riveted. "Your hand . . . "

"Not pretty."

The understatement of the year. Vanessa caught her lower lip between her teeth and bit on it, hard. She wouldn't cry, he hated tears, but her chest felt enclosed in an iron band.

Dominic said roughly: "It'll mend, plastic surgery and all that. I didn't mean you to see it. Don't be upset."

She leaned over him. "I won't cry. I promise."

"Cry all you like. Gerda did and Lucinda screamed the place down when she was hurt."

Gerda and Lucilla! "Who are they?" Vanessa asked.

"My two women in Cyprus. They're flying over to see me so you'll meet them. That is if you want to . . . "

Vanessa dashed a hand across her eyes. "Of course. Is there any reason why I shouldn't?"

"One never quite knows how to please a woman." He sounded weary and Vanessa straightened, aching to kiss him but squashing the desire. Guilt mixed with hurt, she said:

"I've overstayed my limit. Perhaps I shouldn't have come. Oh Dominic, try to be patient. Please. I know all this must be awful after . . . everything else but, at least, you're in a civilised country and safe and . . . we all want you to get better quickly."

She couldn't say any more and felt his eyes following her to the door and knew that somehow, she had failed him.

It was ten days before she visited the hospital again and, this time, because she was summoned to meet his two women from Cyprus. Regular phone calls with Mr Russell had kept her informed of Dominic's progress and she had sent messages to him, but, even so, Vanessa was astonished at the change. He was sitting by the window and, but for the strapped arm and bandaged hand, he looked his old self, slightly arrogant, definitely immaculate, and nothing given away by eyes that could be so expressive.

He had obviously commissioned easy chairs and motioned her and his father to them. To Vanessa he was a stranger, too much in control of himself, too formal, seemingly suffering their presence as a polite necessity.

Then the Perry family arrived, and civilities were exchanged. Gerda appraised Vanessa, and shamelessly kissed Mr Russell. Lucinda dived behind her father's back.

Jon swooped on Dominic in his uninhibited fashion.

"Silly young fool," he said. "I broke my neck to get through to you that the mercenaries had taken over. Why in hell didn't you back out?"

Dominic replied stonily: "I didn't get the message."

Jon tugged at his beard then, with a roughness that plainly expressed his feelings, swung his daughter to his shoulder. Seeming to gain control, he asked: "Have you got rid of Pelham? I hope I don't meet him."

"You won't."

Jon set his struggling daughter down and she approached Dominic warily: "What're you wrapped up for?"

"Fancy dress," he suggested.

"For a party?"

"What party?"

"It's a s'prise and I haven't got to tell you. We're having a party and it's tonight 'cos tomorrow we're going to the boys' school. Daddy's arranged it and he says, if I'm grown up, I can sit next to you."

Dominic said gravely: "I'm honoured."

"Truly?"

"Truly."

Lucinda gave a small shriek and flung herself at him, not hearing Gerda's sharp warning: "You've got your face on but I know it doesn't mean you're cross."

"And you," he said, his look going to Gerda, "are, for once, properly dressed."

Gerda shed her role of propriety and went across to kiss him. "I've shed tears of blood over you, you confounded nuisance. Just marry the beautiful Vanessa and pack up gallivanting all over the world." She glanced swiftly at Vanessa's stiff face and smiled ruefully. "Have I spoken out of turn? Jon'll kill me afterwards. But there's no reason why we shouldn't have a party."

In deference to Dominic's temporary

disability, the meal was held in the Perrys' luxurious hotel suite. It was a pleasant, friendly evening, full of sparkling wit and comical repartee but Dominic tired easily and the ever-watchful Jon called an early halt.

As they left Vanessa heard his bracing reply to Dominic's resentful reference to weakness. "Just stop whining, old son. You're tough and you'll ride this. Advice you won't take, but I might suggest you let your heart rule for a change."

His first personal remark to Vanessa, Dominic made as he was received once more into hospital: "Where are you staying?"

"With your father."

He made no adverse comment but she, sensitive now to his every mood, knew he wasn't pleased. He accepted readmission without another word.

Vanessa couldn't sleep. She had a lot to think about and a lot of blame to accept. Perception told her she was right in believing Dominic disliked the thought of marriage, but she also knew he was the kind of man who would do the right thing, if only for his child.

Do the right thing! She wanted to scream. As if marriage without love had not ruined her teenage years. And this small thing inside her: too young to know and, if the present trend of permissiveness continued, would never really care, that one parent was sacrificing freedom and the other pride.

But it wasn't only pride. She ached for the kind of relationship enjoyed between Gerda and Jon Perry, one of mutual understanding, of deep comradeship, of love in exchanged glances. How she wanted that for herself and Dominic, not a clinical arrangement . . .

The constriction round her chest seemed solid, perhaps, she thought wretchedly, in sympathy with Dominic's crushed ribs.

Dominic. Passionately she wished she had never met him and knew the wish was false.

In the end, Vanessa left the warmth of her bed and padded round the cold room. It was Dominic's, Mr Russell had told her so, vaguely commenting that they didn't maintain the guest-room as it was rarely used. 'Dominic's is more habitable,' he'd said.

Vanessa didn't think the room was habitable. She thought it bare and unhospitable, not liking her presence in the least — a ridiculous assumption but one she couldn't shake off. My nerves, she thought, are shot to pieces. I must take a grip on them and try to think positively.

The only positive action was to bury her inclinations and marry Dominic . . . providing he asked her again after being so summarily rebuffed.

Vanessa grimaced at her wan reflection in the severe-looking mirror. She must make allowances for the abrupt, insensitive proposal from a man who was far from his normal self. He might not remember or, now out of sedation, regret the uncharacteristic impulse.

She opened drawers one by one. All tidy and sparsely filled with clothing from Dominic's younger days: school and college ties, sports gear, everything orderly. In the last drawer, letters and photographs.

Vanessa closed the drawer with a slam and crawled, shivering, into bed, her one wish to get the night over. Behind her heavy lids she saw the closing sentence of the uppermost letter:

'It will be many years before we meet again, my dearest son. Don't forget me. Myriads of love. Your true father.'

13

HE was standing on the plateau just as she had always thought of him: straight-backed, immaculate, expressionless as he appraised her. Knowing her waistline had thickened and her face was pale, she stopped, embarrassed, no other feeling penetrating the daily lethargy that seemed to be a part of her life.

Dominic stepped forward, his hold firm as he helped her over the last and steepest climb. Voice modulated, he said: "I shall have to extract a promise from you, young Meredith, but as it's your birthday, we'll leave it for now." With an almost unscarred hand he gestured to the mist, dancing in small spirals over the heather. "A warning."

Vanessa roused herself to protest: "There's a breeze."

"That can drop in an instant."

His touch was dissolving something inside her, the rigid self-control, the fear of the future, the burden of lonely responsibility. He had gone away for a month and, characteristically, had returned a week early. Still a law unto himself. They had spoken over the telephone and exchanged difficult letters. He had sent her a ring which she hadn't worn. Apparently she hadn't changed either, still stubborn and impulsive with a blind disregard of advice, hearing but never heeding.

Dominic said into the tense silence: "I've been summoned, once again, to shoulder my responsibilities."

"Georgina."

"Not this time. Father."

"But you needed a holiday."

"Holiday in a Swiss health farm? I've saved the holiday to share with you."

They came then, the pent-up tears of many long weeks, rending, soul-revealing, cleansing and then, held in gentle warmth, blessedly relieving.

A shoulder to cry on!

Dominic said comically: "You've soaked my shirt."

He hated a woman to cry. Vanessa moved her face to a dry spot and received a spotless white handkerchief. She gave a weak laugh through her hiccups. Trust Dominic to produce the right equipment, always clean. He would turn up clean from a mud bath. It was many years before she learned the whole story of his ordeal in Beirut and then it came from Jon.

He asked: "Better now?"

"Yes. I'm sorry. I know you despise tears."

"Do I? You have that wrong. Tears scare me. I don't know how to deal with them and you have just proved the point."

He had proved other things too. Vanessa looked up and saw the mist descending. "Dominic."

"It's all right. I know every inch of this hill. We'll go back to the house ... slowly ... and hope lunch is ready."

Unhappily aware of her blotched face, Vanessa kept her head turned from him, mumbling guiltily: "I haven't done anything about food yet."

"I have. After tearing up her latest lurid manuscript, Georgina promised a session in the kitchen. She's not too bad a cook if over-spiced stuff appeals."

Half an hour later, Vanessa had showered, half dressed and was vigorously brushing her hair, when Dominic walked into her room. It would have been ridiculous for her to object to the familiarity but her cheeks burned nevertheless and he eyed them with interest as he sat on the wide window-sill.

"You aren't wearing my ring," he observed.

"No."

"Where is it?"

Still flustered she said without thinking: "In the bottom drawer." Then, as he got up and realisation came, she made swift protest: "No! Leave it. I'll get it in a minute."

He stopped, dark brows raised: "Secrets?"

"No." Her face burned more than ever: "Don't rush me. I didn't expect you ... I ... " He didn't retreat and his proximity set her pulses racing. It was easier to give way than to betray her need. Bending down she opened the drawer, lifted out the small box and handed it to him, then found his gaze was riveted to the neat piles of small garments.

"When," he asked, "did you buy those?"

"I didn't buy them, I made them." Why did she sound so defiant, as if she were ashamed of the confession.

"How on earth did you find the time? I understand Georgina has been a slave-driver and that a great deal of your time has been taken up with trying to eliminate yourself."

"What nonsense. Your spies exaggerated, Mr — "

He cut her off sharply: "Don't you dare call me that unless you'd like a slap." Lips pulling he bent to place a light kiss on her nose. "Don't worry, I wouldn't. Don't let me scare you, Vanessa. I don't mean to. You'll have to give me a few sharp lessons on the correct way to handle a little lady. Gerda rubbed in a few home truths and now it's up to you. Now tell me when you so industriously make clothes for the baby and then hide them away?"

"When I can't sleep." Vanessa threw down the brush she was gripping so tightly, upsetting a bottle of unstoppered perfume. "Knitting is soporific." She watched as he righted the bottle, replacing the top. The surgeon had worked a miracle with the raw wounds and only the nails needed more time to recover. She shuddered inwardly at what Dominic must have suffered. He was tough, so everyone said, but there must be a limit to what a man can endure.

He said in her ear: "Come back to

earth. What are you thinking about?"

"Nothing I can tell you, not now anyway. D'you want to look at the Russell brat's future attire?" Whether he did or not she didn't wait to hear, handing him the carefully folded clothing. "To baby with love."

He walked away abruptly, his back to her as he spread coats, leggings and tiny tops over the bed. "Is this all they wear?" His tone was gruff.

"No, but I could hardly provide vests in apple green."

"Why have you used apple green, so much of it?"

She had the feeling he was making conversation to cover embarrassment, but after she had told him about the wool in the attic, he asked, a curt edge to his voice: "Are you short of money?"

"Sort of. Georgina pays me when she remembers I'm an employee."

He swung around: "So you have bought nothing for yourself?"

"Not since the dress you disliked."

Avoiding his gaze she added, a trifle defensively: "I haven't needed anything. Clothes may be your priority but they aren't mine."

He laughed, disarming her completely: "I don't mind being your whipping boy as long as you don't make too much of a habit of turning me inside out. I think it's my turn, but it is your birthday so I'll shelve it. All I'm asking is for you to be ready in about an hour. We're going into town to celebrate."

Vanessa didn't ask why, she was too busy revelling in the rapid uplift of spirits. She said, matching his tone: "I'll be ready in the dress that makes me look ninety. At least you like that. And I shan't be longer than fifteen minutes."

Outside the chauffeur was waiting in Mr Russell's limousine. "Manning will deliver and collect, easier for shopping, and quicker, not too much walking about for you."

She was being cosseted for the first time in her life. As Dominic sat beside her, she turned to look at him, knowing her eyes were wide with speculation, giving away her disbelief in this sudden change of circumstances.

He smiled but didn't speak, simply reached out to turn her face to the window and it was in this soothing silence that they travelled most of the way. Remembering the hectic shopping spree with Georgina, Vanessa was still not prepared for the speed of the next few hours. Exhausted but exhilarated, she eventually found herself alone in a hotel room with an astonishing number of boxes stacked neatly inside the door.

She was still unpacking when Dominic came into the room and without turning round she challenged: "You paid for all these, so come and choose what I'm to wear for dinner." He was at the cabinet, pouring drinks and she prompted: "Which dress?"

"I haven't the slightest idea, not being accustomed to choosing ladies' clothes."

"You didn't do so badly in the boutiques."

"I chose at random. Maybe the colour."

Not believing, she exclaimed: "You humbug, Mr Russell, sir."

He said sharply: "*Don't* call me that."

"You call me young Meredith." She appraised his taut face and said impulsively: "You've tired yourself out. I appreciate you coming home and all you have done for me but . . ." About to ask why he had, she changed direction, "You should have stayed the course in Switzerland."

He handed over her glass. "I was sick of it, sick of being organised. I stayed three weeks because of the pure air." He regarded her ominously: "What's so funny . . . and don't say 'nothing'."

"I wasn't going to. No comment."

Surprisingly, he bent to drop a light kiss on her lips. "At least you're original. You don't pander or pontificate."

To hide her embarrassment, Vanessa turned pointedly to the array of new garments and demanded: "Which dress?"

"Does it matter? The one you like best."

"How aggravating you can be. It matters to you what you wear. Even a penguin suit must have the right width of lapel and a trendy cut. If I prance into the dining-room in my new underwear it'd matter. Or wouldn't you notice?"

The tightness of his mouth relaxed. Reaching past her he tapped the dress she secretly preferred. "This one. Now are you satisfied?"

She was, very, excitement high inside her, the lethargy of the past weeks forgotten. Strange, she had never realised what a difference a new dress could make. And the other things . . . ridiculous, fabulously expensive and sheer bliss to the skin. She said and knew she was being childish: "I want to shower and get dressed up. How long have I got?"

He was still faintly smiling: "I'll come for you about eight. Don't forget your drink."

She did, but the supply was plentiful over the meal, reminiscent of the party night when Dominic had seduced her. Was he paving the way once more? she wondered. Perhaps he would ask her again to marry him. This time she'd accept; certainly she didn't want to bring the awful darkness to his eyes.

He was studying the menu and she studied him, suddenly afraid as she'd been afraid for so long. Did she know him well enough to take such a final step? Did she know all of his moods or did the guard that changed the colour of his eyes, hide more than she could fathom? Could she survive the uncertainty of not knowing what he was hiding?

"Dominic," she said.

He looked up and his eyes were very blue. "Shall I choose for you? Something light!" As she nodded he read out his choice and she nodded again, not really enthusiastic. But when the food came it was good and she enjoyed every morsel, surprised that he ate so little. Keeping his weight down, she thought, yet he had no surplus as far as she could see. Why had her bubbling confidence deserted? Would she ever have the courage to demand his confidence. She had seen him in despair, angry, petulant as a little boy, in pain, and had been the recipient of his officiousness.

She had also, that day, known his protective instinct and — an age ago it seemed — the intimacy of his touch, incredibly gentle.

Dominic said quietly: "It's time you were in bed. I'll see you to your room and then I'm going for a walk."

About to protest, Vanessa thought better of it and he added with the faintly amused undertone she was getting to know: "Later I'll kiss you goodnight . . . that is, if you aren't asleep."

She wasn't, although she feigned sleep, watching through half-closed eyelashes his soft-footed approach and seeing him as on that night before, clad in silk pyjamas, dressing-gown slung across his shoulders.

"Do you always bury that ridiculous nose?" he asked. "Come up for air, or is this hide-and-seek?"

She came up for air and he kissed her, lightly and teasingly giving no promise and no satisfaction. Vanessa turned her face away, denying her inner trembling, aching for more and wishing she didn't love him, that she could tell him to go, preserving her pride.

I need him, she thought, and was horrified at the threat of tears. Dear heaven, not a second time. Hearing her own choked voice, she said: "You should be in bed too. It's been a heavy day . . . after the health farm."

"Don't you believe it."

She tried again: "All the same — "

He cut in, sharp with self-mockery: "It would be too humiliating if I ran out of breath."

Vanessa sat up, narrowly missing his chin. "You . . . you idiot, your breathing's fine."

"It was until I met the fumes dear London has to offer."

She said irrelevantly: "The champagne has gone to my head, delayed action. You make me drink it purposely and now you're going to waste it."

"You little devil." He pushed her down and she teased him about the awful shame of running out of breath.

His mouth was possessive now. "I'll risk it," he murmured to her breast. "Something from you first: will you marry me?"

She had spoken truly about the champagne: "For young Russell's sake, I will. I'm told that money paves the way if there's not enough love." Feeling him stiffen she put a cheek to his hair: "I've plenty for the two of us and it'll last a lifetime . . . sort of makes things even."

"Even be damned," he exploded. "The feeling I have inside burns me up. What is there about this marriage lark anyway?"

Vanessa mentally embraced the future.

He would go away again because he was made that way. But he would always return. Half to herself she murmured sleepily: "For us both, my dear Dominic, simply a shoulder to cry on. We'll have each other."

THE END

WITH SOMEBODY ELSE
Theresa Charles

Rosamond sets off for Cornwall with Hugo to meet his family, blissfully unaware of the shocks in store for her.

A SUMMER FOR STRANGERS
Claire Hamilton

Because she had lost her job, her flat and she had no money, Tabitha agreed to pose as Adam's future wife although she believed the scheme to be deceitful and cruel.

VILLA OF SINGING WATER
Angela Petron

The disquieting incidents that occurred at the Vatican and the Colosseum did not trouble Jan at first, but then they became increasingly unpleasant and alarming.

DOCTOR NAPIER'S NURSE
Pauline Ash

When cousins Midge and Derry are entered as probationer nurses on the same day but at different hospitals they agree to exchange identities.

A GIRL LIKE JULIE
Louise Ellis

Caroline absolutely adored Hugh Barrington, but then Julie Crane came into their lives. Julie was the kind of girl who attracts men without even trying.

COUNTRY DOCTOR
Paula Lindsay

When Evan Richmond bought a practice in a remote country village he did not realise that a casual encounter would lead to the loss of his heart.

ENCORE
Helga Moray

Craig and Janet realise that their true happiness lies with each other, but it is only under traumatic circumstances that they can be reunited.

NICOLETTE
Ivy Preston

When Grant Alston came back into her life, Nicolette was faced with a dilemma. Should she follow the path of duty or the path of love?

THE GOLDEN PUMA
Margaret Way

Catherine's time was spent looking after her father's Queensland farm. But what life was there without David, who wasn't interested in her?

HOSPITAL BY THE LAKE
Anne Durham

Nurse Marguerite Ingleby was always ready to become personally involved with her patients, to the despair of Brian Field, the Senior Surgical Registrar, who loved her.

VALLEY OF CONFLICT
David Farrell

Isolated in a hostel in the French Alps, Ann Russell sees her fiancé being seduced by a young girl. Then comes the avalanche that imperils their lives.

NURSE'S CHOICE
Peggy Gaddis

A proposal of marriage from the incredibly handsome and wealthy Reagan was enough to upset any girl — and Brooke Martin was no exception.

A DANGEROUS MAN
Anne Goring

Photographer Polly Burton was on safari in Mombasa when she met enigmatic Leon Hammond. But unpredictability was the name of the game where Leon was concerned.

PRECIOUS INHERITANCE
Joan Moules

Karen's new life working for an authoress took her from Sussex to a foreign airstrip and a kidnapping; to a real life adventure as gripping as any in the books she typed.

VISION OF LOVE
Grace Richmond

When Kathy takes over the rundown country kennels she finds Alec Stinton, a local vet, very helpful. But their friendship arouses bitter jealousy and a tragedy seems inevitable.

CRUSADING NURSE
Jane Converse

It was handsome Dr. Corbett who opened Nurse Susan Leighton's eyes and who set her off on a lonely crusade against some powerful enemies and a shattering struggle against the man she loved.

WILD ENCHANTMENT
Christina Green

Rowan's agreeable new boss had a dream of creating a famous perfume using her precious Silverstar, but Rowan's plans were very different.

DESERT ROMANCE
Irene Ord

Sally agrees to take her sister Pam's place as La Chartreuse the dancer, but she finds out there is more to it than dyeing her hair red and looking like her sister.

HEART OF ICE
Marie Sidney

How was January to know that not only would the warmth of the Swiss people thaw out her frozen heart, but that she too would play her part in helping someone to live again?

LUCKY IN LOVE
Margaret Wood

Companion-secretary to wealthy gambler Laura Duxford, who lived in Monaco, seemed to Melanie a fabulous job. Especially as Melanie had already lost her heart to Laura's son, Julian.

NURSE TO PRINCESS JASMINE
Lilian Woodward

Nick's surgeon brother, Tom, performs an operation on an Arabian princess, and she invites Tom, Nick and his fiancé to Omander, where a web of deceit and intrigue closes about them.

THE WAYWARD HEART
Eileen Barry

Disaster-prone Katherine's nickname was "Kate Calamity", but her boss went too far with an outrageous proposal, which because of her latest disaster, she could not refuse.

FOUR WEEKS IN WINTER
Jane Donnelly

Tessa wasn't looking forward to meeting Paul Mellor again — she had made a fool of herself over him once before. But was Orme Jared's solution to her problem likely to be the right one?

SURGERY BY THE SEA
Sheila Douglas

Medical student Meg hadn't really wanted to go and work with a G.P. on the Welsh coast although the job had its compensations. But Owen Roberts was certainly not one of them!

HEAVEN IS HIGH
Anne Hampson

The new heir to the Manor of Marbeck had been found. But it was rather unfortunate that when he arrived unexpectedly he found an uninvited guest, complete with stetson and high boots.

LOVE WILL COME
Sarah Devon

June Baker's boss was not really her idea of her ideal man, but when she went from third typist to boss's secretary overnight she began to change her mind.

ESCAPE TO ROMANCE
Kay Winchester

Oliver and Jean first met on Swale Island. They were both trying to begin their lives afresh, but neither had bargained for complications from the past.

CASTLE IN THE SUN
Cora Mayne

Emma's invalid sister, Kym, needed a warm climate, and Emma jumped at the chance of a job on a Mediterranean island. But Emma soon finds that intrigues and hazards lurk on the sunlit isle.

BEWARE OF LOVE
Kay Winchester

Carol Brampton resumes her nursing career when her family is killed in a car accident. With Dr. Patrick Farrell she begins to pick up the pieces of her life, but is bitterly hurt when insinuations are made about her to Patrick.

DARLING REBEL
Sarah Devon

When Jason Farradale's secretary met with an accident, her glamorous stand-in was quite unable to deal with one problem in particular.

THE PRICE OF PARADISE
Jane Arbor

It was a shock to Fern to meet her estranged husband on an island in the middle of the Indian Ocean, but to discover that her father had engineered it puzzled Fern. What did he hope to achieve?

DOCTOR IN PLASTER
Lisa Cooper

When Dr. Scott Sutcliffe is injured, Nurse Caroline Hurst has to cope with a very demanding private case. But when she realises her exasperating patient has stolen her heart, how can Caroline possibly stay?

A TOUCH OF HONEY
Lucy Gillen

Before she took the job as secretary to author Robert Dean, Cadie had heard how charming he was, but that wasn't her first impression at all.

ROMANTIC LEGACY
Cora Mayne

As kennelmaid to the Armstrongs, Ann Brown, had no idea that she would become the central figure in a web of mystery and intrigue.

THE RELENTLESS TIDE
Jill Murray

Steve Palmer shared Nurse Marie Blane's love of the sea and small boats. Marie's other passion was her step-brother. But when danger threatened who should she turn to — her step-brother or the man who stirred emotions in her heart?

ROMANCE IN NORWAY
Cora Mayne

Nancy Crawford hopes that her visit to Norway will help her to start life again. She certainly finds many surprises there, including unexpected happiness.

UNLOCK MY HEART
Honor Vincent

When Ruth Linton, a young widow with three children, inherits a house in the country, it seems to be the answer to her dreams. But Ruth's problems were only just beginning . . .

SWEET PROMISE
Janet Dailey

Erica had met Rafael in Mexico, where their relationship had been brief but dramatic. Now, over a year later in Texas, she had met him again — and he had the power to wreck her life.

SAFARI ENCOUNTER
Rosemary Carter

Jenny had to accept that she couldn't run her father's game park alone; so she let forceful Joshua Adams virtually take over. But Joshua took over her heart as well!

1		25		49		73	8/08	
2	4/11	26		50		74		
3		27		51		75		
4		28		52		76		
5	10/13	29		53		77		
6		30	11/8	54		78		
7		31	12/10	55		79		
8		32		56		80		
9		33		57	4/8	81		
10	·	34		58		82		
11		35		59		83		
12		36		60		84		
13	8/14	37		61	4/09	85		
14		38		62	10/16	86		
15		39		63		87		
16		40		64		88		
17		41		65		89		
18		42		66		90		
19		43		67		91		
20		44		68	5/19	92		
21		45	8/09	69		COMMUNITY SERVICES		
22	7/07	46	2/09	70				
23		47	4/13	71		NPT/111		
24		48		72				

TENDER DECEPTION

Laura P...

...ton was taken fi... Workhouse to be a s... at Perriman Court, h... looked bleak. Was it really a... Providence that persuaded Lady Perriman to adopt her as her ward? Sophia was brought up together with the Perriman children, and before sailing with his regiment for India, George, the heir to the title, declared his love. But tragedy hit the family and Sophia found herself caught up in a web of mystery and intrigue.

THE SOLDIER'S WOMAN

Freda M. Long

When Lieutenant Alain d'Albert was deserted by his girlfriend, a replacement was at hand in the shape of Christina Calvi, whose yearning for respectability through marriage did not quite coincide with her profession as a soldier's woman. Christina's obsessive love for Alain was not returned. The handsome hussar married an heiress and banished the soldier's woman from his life. But Christina was unswerving in the pursuit of her dream and Alain found his resistance weakening . . .